THE SPEED OF DEATH

The major's hand flew toward his right hip and the six-gun holstered there. Slocum had seen faster men, but he couldn't remember when. He went for his own gun, and the world seemed to turn to molasses around him. He saw the major's Colt Army clear leather and start to center on him. Slocum's hand closed on the ebony butt of his six-shooter, but try as he might, he couldn't force any more speed out of his draw.

He was going to die.

DON'T MISS THESE
ALL-ACTION WESTERN SERIES
FROM THE BERKLEY PUBLISHING GROUP

THE GUNSMITH by J. R. Roberts
Clint Adams was a legend among lawmen, outlaws, and ladies. They called him . . . the Gunsmith.

LONGARM by Tabor Evans
The popular long-running series about U.S. Deputy Marshal Long—his life, his loves, his fight for justice.

LONE STAR by Wesley Ellis
The blazing adventures of Jessica Starbuck and the martial arts master, Ki. Over eight million copies in print.

SLOCUM by Jake Logan
Today's longest-running action western. John Slocum rides a deadly trail of hot blood and cold steel.

JAKE LOGAN

REVENGE AT DEVILS TOWER

BERKLEY BOOKS, NEW YORK

REVENGE AT DEVILS TOWER

A Berkley Book / published by arrangement with the author

PRINTING HISTORY
Berkley edition / September 1993

ISBN: 0-425-13904-2

A BERKLEY BOOK ® TM 757,375
Berkley Books are published by The Berkley Publishing Group,
200 Madison Avenue, New York, New York 10016.
The name "BERKLEY" and the "B" logo
are trademarks belonging to Berkley Publishing Corporation.

PRINTED IN THE UNITED STATES OF AMERICA

10 9 8 7 6 5 4 3 2 1

REVENGE AT DEVILS TOWER

1

"Stampede!"

John Slocum jerked around to find who had shouted. After six weeks on the Western Trail to Dodge City from Texas, he had come to rely on the other cowboys as if they were brothers. Nobody would joke about something this dire.

And no one was joshing now. The shout came again—and Slocum felt the earth begin to rumble under his horse's hooves. He patted the mare's neck and tried to soothe her. It didn't work. Her nostrils flared and her eyes showed white rims. The horse knew the danger of twelve hundred head of longhorns running out of control.

"Where?" Slocum called. "Where's the herd?"

The land in Kansas was mostly flat, but this section had more than its share of ravines and rolling hills. Slocum had been working his way down a sandy draw hunting for strays. He fought to get his horse moving up the ravine's bank to higher ground.

No matter what happened, he didn't want to be caught in the draw. A spooked herd was as likely to plunge over the side and crush anything—and anyone—below them as they were to run themselves to exhaustion. The only way Slocum could see to get the herd turned and break the panic seizing the steers was to be out on the plains. And if he couldn't turn the herd, he wanted to be able to get the hell out of the way.

His horse slipped in the sandy soil and tried to shy. Slocum kept the mare moving and got to the top of the embankment. The dust cloud rising a mile off showed where the danger lay.

"Them damned cows are headin' for that sodbuster's spread," shouted Rusty Neal from a dozen yards away. "What do we do, Slocum? I ain't gettin' between them and dyin' for no sodbuster."

Slocum's keen green eyes judged distances and the speed of the herd. The stampede was building power. The ground rolled under him as if an earthquake shook the world, and the dust kicked up by hooves was as fierce as any West Texas sandstorm. Rusty Neal was right about not wanting to get in front of that charging wall of mindless muscle and meat.

"We could never get close enough to do much good," Slocum said. "That farmer's place is going under, no matter what." Slocum pulled out a short spyglass from his saddlebags and peered through it. He went cold inside when he saw the real danger.

The cowboys in Bill Granger's employ were clear of the herd. None of them would get trampled if the herd was allowed to run itself into the ground. The sodbuster's wife and three children weren't so lucky. Slocum damned them for being out on the prairie where they didn't belong. Whatever had taken the four away from their sod house was also going to be the cause of their death.

"How far do you make it, Rusty?" Slocum asked, pulling out his Winchester and dropping to the ground.

"You ain't got a chance of dropping the leader, Slocum. It's more'n a mile!"

Slocum didn't see that he had much choice. He wished he had a Sharps .50 or some other heavy caliber rifle. Knocking down a steer wasn't much different from potshotting buffalo if you had the right weapon for the job. Slocum touched the front sight of his rifle and knew that a .44-40 bullet didn't have much stopping power at this range.

He dropped to his belly and levered in a round. He saw from the cloud of dust being kicked high into the air that it was a still, hot Kansas day. That made windage correction less of a worry than just getting the bullet thrown out to the right distance. During the war he had been a sniper—one of the best—but he had always waited for the perfect shot. And humans had been much smaller targets.

He fired. The first round kicked up dust a score of feet too short of his target. Slocum quickly corrected and fired.

"I think you got one, Slocum. That steer up front stumbled a mite," reported Rusty Neal. The cowboy pushed back his broad-brimmed, sil-belly Stetson and peered through Slocum's spyglass.

He let out a whoop of joy when Slocum's second, third, and fourth bullets ripped into the steers at the front of the stampede.

"One's slowing," Neal reported. "The son of a bitch fell!"

Slocum kept firing until the magazine was empty, then he reloaded and fired again. More shots missed than hit, but the sound of the rifle was having its effect on the panicked cattle as much as the rounds that found tough hides to pierce. Slocum fired and fired until white smoke filled the air in front of him, choking him something fierce. Now he wished for a little breeze.

"What of the woman and her kids?" Slocum asked. He loaded the last few rounds he had, wondering if he was accomplishing anything other than wasting ammunition.

"They got smart and went to ground," Neal said, swinging the spyglass around. "I see the woman's head. They're hunkered down behind a small rise."

Slocum rolled over and got a better view of the herd. Some of the steam had been taken out of the stampede when the leading steers started stumbling with Slocum's bullets in them. Several fell and got kicked to death by the tons of beef rushing behind. The falling steers had turned the herd just enough to give some hope for the sodbuster woman and her brood.

"That did it," Rusty Neal shouted, jumping up and down. "That did the trick." The cowboy came over and slapped Slocum on the shoulder.

"Let's go see if the woman's all right," Slocum said, wincing as he burned himself on the rifle's hot barrel. He would find a gunsmith when they got to Dodge City. The heat might have melted the barrel out of true aim.

Slocum and Neal mounted and rode toward the spot where the woman still cowered with her three children. She looked up with eyes wide with fear. Seeing Slocum and Neal, the fear changed to anger.

"You get off our land!" she raged. "Take those Texas fever–infested steer cows with you! How dare you risk our lives!"

"But ma'am, Slocum here's the one what turned the stampede. They would have stomped you and yours into the ground something fierce," Rusty Neal pointed out. Slocum saw that the woman wasn't up to listening to reason.

"We got work to do," he told Neal.

"But, John, this here lady's got it all wrong. You *saved* her!"

"When my husband gets out here, he'll take a bullwhip to your worthless hides!" the woman shouted.

Slocum and Rusty Neal rode off, letting the woman shout insults at their backs.

"How's that for gratitude?" Neal asked, shaking his head. "You done her a favor, and she gets all fired up."

"People around here need us but surely don't like seeing us come to their town." Slocum fell silent and looked at the damage done. Bill Granger might have to deal with the woman's husband about the destruction the herd had caused. Two gardens and a patch of alfalfa had been all dug up by the stampede, but the woman and her children were safe. Slocum just hoped Granger saw it that way.

Shooting four or five head might not go down well with the trail boss. If that came out of Slocum's pay, he'd have spent the last six weeks on the trail for nothing.

"Slocum, Neal, glad you decided to get your asses back here," Granger growled. "We got to drive those dumb cows around this here homesteader's place." He jerked his thumb over his shoulder in the direction of the sod house where the woman shouted at a man Slocum took to be her husband.

"You have to pay for the damage?" Slocum asked.

"He took fifty dollars and kept the five head that got killed." Bill Granger let out a huge sigh. "I'm so glad we're almost at Dodge City I could piss champagne. This has been the worst drive yet."

"You're gettin' too old for this, boss," piped up Rusty Neal. The look he got silenced the red-haired man. Slocum knew better than to comment when the trail boss started bitching and moaning. This was his way of letting off steam. Others Slocum had ridden with took out their frustration on their men, sometimes with fists, and other times with knives and six-guns. Granger was better than that—if you let him be when he got to ranting.

Slocum and the other cowboys rounded up the strays lagging the herd, and then got the longhorns moving in the direction of Dodge City. They found the feedlots an hour before sundown.

"Get those miserable beeves into that pen!" Granger shouted. He took off his hat and waved it above his head, letting out a loud yell.

Slocum shared the trail boss's delight in finishing the drive. He needed a hot bath, a good meal, and not just a little bit of whiskey. And since Granger had said nothing about shooting the longhorns to turn the stampede, Slocum would get his full fifty dollars.

"Boys, come on back when you got a hankering to ride the trail with me again. You're about the best danged crew I've ever seen," Granger said as he paid them their wages.

"And this from a man who thought it was his worst drive ever," grumbled Rusty Neal. But the redhead counted his money, tucked it into his shirt pocket, and lit out for town without so much as a backward look. The others followed him, leaving behind Slocum and Granger.

"Slocum," the trail boss said. His eyes bored into Slocum.

"What is it?" Slocum was prepared for just about anything, including the demand to turn over his pay for killing the rampaging cattle.

"This was a good crew of cowboys, and you're the best of the lot. Come on back to the Panhandle with me. The X Bar X needs men year-round. We can pay top dollar."

"I'll think on it," Slocum said. He had eaten enough dust for now, and if he never saw another cow that wasn't cut up and sizzling on a dinner platter, it'd be three days too soon.

"Thanks for getting that stampede turned the way you did. Those sodbusters might not appreciate it, but I do. Hate explaining to the law in these cow towns how their citizens got run down by a longhorn." Granger turned and walked off without another word. He knew if Slocum accepted his offer of employment he would be back.

If not, to hell with him.

Slocum was inclined to drift farther north; after a bath and shave, a decent meal, and enough whiskey to float a riverboat.

The town sported a half dozen barbershops, and Slocum found one willing to pour him a gallon of steaming-hot water and give him a shave for only a dollar. He changed into his spare clothes and felt a world better for it. He rubbed his belly and went looking for a good café. The gambling houses lining Dodge City's Front Street drew him, as did the sound of cowboys inside knocking back hard, harsh liquor, but Slocum had been on the trail too long not to appreciate hot food. The Alhambra or the Long Branch could wait a spell longer.

In a wide-open and accommodating town like Dodge, there was always time for gambling, drinking, and maybe even finding a willing woman, if he had two coins left to jingle.

Slocum was choosy about the place where he ate, and he had the money riding in his shirt pocket to have his druthers. Several places looked decent enough but were filled with rowdy cowboys. Slocum avoided them and walked away from the main streets into the quieter sections of town. He found a secluded café that sported a decent menu. He went in and got a once-over from the café owner. Slocum was clean enough to pass muster, and was shown to a table by the front window. He sat and took his time ordering. This increased his rapt anticipation of the porterhouse steak smothered in onions with all the fixings. By the time it came he was about ready to rip it apart with his teeth.

Slocum cut each piece with surgical precision and ate slowly, savoring the taste. On the trail they only got the steers that had died. Otherwise, it was mostly salt pork and beans, with dried peas, and occasional cans of peaches to break the monotony.

He paused, another forkful halfway to his mouth. A noise in the street caught his attention. He saw a pretty woman—tall, slender, with chestnut hair all aflutter—backing down the boardwalk. She held out her arms, as though trying to shove someone away.

As she passed his vantage point, Slocum saw the problem. Two drunk cowboys were annoying the woman. Her eyes were wide, reminding Slocum of the way his mare's eyes had been when the sound of the stampede filled the prairie.

The difference was obvious, though. The horse had had room to run—and the woman was far prettier.

Slocum finished the morsel of steak on his fork and watched a bit longer. This wasn't his fight. He didn't know the woman, and the law in Dodge City didn't take kindly to cowboys breezing into their town and shooting it up. Now and again drovers tried to hurrah Dodge, and they usually ended up in the hoosegow.

But this was different. The sheriff was nowhere to be seen and no one, least of all a man born and raised in Georgia, was going to allow a woman to be set upon. Slocum reached over and slipped the leather thong off the hammer of his Colt Navy. He had checked the six-shooter before coming into Dodge City, so he knew it had a full load.

"Be right back," Slocum said, getting up and putting on his hat.

"You finished?" asked the waiter, eyeing Slocum as if he thought he was going to run out on the bill.

"Not quite. A piece of apple cobbler sounds like an outstanding way to finish the meal."

"But—"

Slocum ran through the door when the woman let out a squeal of pain. One of the cowboys had grabbed her upper arm and flung her against the post holding up the roof over the boardwalk.

"Come on now, you want what I got to offer."

"Please, sir, you're hurting me. Let me go." The brunette's words carried spirit, fire, and enough of a bite to let Slocum know she would fight if she had to.

He slammed hard into the second cowboy, knocking him ass over teakettle across the railing. The man spun around and landed hard in the dusty street.

"Pleasant evening, isn't it, ma'am?" Slocum said, tipping his hat politely. He never took his eyes off the man annoying the woman.

"Slick, he knocked me down!" complained the man in the street. He was so drunk and tangled up he couldn't get his feet and arms working right. Slocum saw he wasn't likely to find the hogleg slung on his hip anytime soon, either. The real danger lay in the man holding the woman's arm.

"This ain't your concern, mister," the one called Slick snarled. He turned just enough for the woman to jerk free.

"Run on along, Miss," said Slocum. His cold green eyes bored into Slick's hot brown ones.

"You ain't the law," Slick said.

"He ain't?" piped up his companion. From the corner of his eye Slocum saw the man in the street getting to his feet and going for his six-gun. Slocum took a quick step to the side, drew his gun and swung it as hard as he could, buffaloing the man.

The sick crunch as metal hit the side of his head echoed louder than any gunshot. The man sank to the street, unconscious.

But as Slocum turned back, he saw he had miscalculated. Slick hadn't just gone for his gun, he had grabbed the woman and pulled her in front of him as a shield.

"What you gonna do now?" Slick snarled.

Slocum put his Colt back into the cross-draw holster and stepped out into the street. In a voice colder than a blue norther, he said, "I'm going to wait for you to come out here and face me like a man."

Slocum saw the fright on the woman's face, and he saw that Slick wasn't going to make this a fair fight. The cowboy's thumb rubbed nervously on the hammer of his six-shooter, then pulled it back.

The cocking pistol sounded like the gates of hell squeaking open. It was time for someone to die.

2

Slocum knew he had to be careful. One slip and the drunk cowboy would squeeze off a round through the woman's head.

With his eyes on Slick, Slocum waited for just a moment. Then he made a feint to the left, swinging his head and shoulders in that direction. A quick jerk sent him flying to the right and at the same time his hand was moving to his Colt Navy. The trick worked.

Slick tried to follow Slocum's movement with the muzzle of his gun. The instant it veered from the woman's head, she acted. Stamping down hard with her foot, she got in a good blow to the cowboy's boot. Then the brunette reared back and kicked him hard in the shins. This caused him to recoil and move back from her.

Slocum's bullet caught him square in the chest. Slick looked surprised, then folded like a bad poker hand.

The shot was hardly audible amid the furor coming from Front Street. Drovers were shooting up the saloons and gambling halls, and reports from six-shooters and the tinkling of shattered glass were almost too loud to be tolerated.

The woman stood and stared at Slick's motionless body, then her wide brown eyes moved in Slocum's direction.

Her mouth opened and closed but no sound came out. Slocum took a quick look in the direction of the man he had buffaloed. He was still out cold.

"I've got a cup of coffee waiting inside," Slocum said. "Reckon it's getting cold. When they freshen it up, they can get you one, too, if I might be so bold as to offer."

"Why, yes, of course," the woman said, finding her voice. Her lips moved again, but Slocum didn't hear what she was saying. Together they went into the café and returned to Slocum's table. The owner was standing to one side, in a position to have clearly seen all that happened outside.

"You done good, mister," the owner said. "That good-for-nothing snake's been nothing but trouble since he blowed into town a week ago. He even walked out on his bill!"

The way the man had said it, Slocum wondered if there was any worse crime.

"Coffee for the lady," he said.

"Please, no." She swallowed hard. "Can I have a cup of tea instead?"

"Coffee for me, tea for the lady—and where's the apple cobbler?"

"Didn't know if you'd still want it," the café owner said insincerely. Slocum read him like a book. When Slocum had left the cafe, everyone inside had thought Slocum was going to get his head shot off. Now, nobody paid him any attention, some even pointedly ignored him and the woman.

"My name's John Slocum," he introduced.

"You killed him," she said in a weak voice. "I don't believe I ever saw anyone killed before. Except old Mr. Johnson, but that was different. He fell from his porch, but he was old and. . . ." Her eyes snapped away from where Slick lay and fixed on Slocum.

"I do carry on, don't I?" she asked, her voice gathering some strength.

"Where back East are you from?" Slocum asked. "By your accent I'd say you hail from Boston. Or maybe New York."

She was smiling more now and the color was coming back into her cheeks. "You have a good ear for accents."

"And you have a way of avoiding a man's question," Slocum pointed out. He accepted his coffee and the apple cobbler. He set to eating the fruit before he forgot what it tasted like. It had been too long since he'd had anything that was fresh.

"I am sorry. I'm from New York. My name is Ruth Waddell. I only arrived in Dodge City this morning."

"Train?" Slocum asked between bites and gulps.

"Why, yes. From Kansas City. How did you know?" Ruth Waddell looked as if she had never considered anyone might be able to figure out a young girl from New York had to pass through a major railhead to get to the edge of civilization, if Dodge City could be mentioned in the same breath with any sophisticated metropolis.

Slocum shrugged. He was getting to the point where he would pop if he ate any more. He finished his coffee. Ruth barely sampled her tea. Slocum didn't fault her for that. The ugly brown liquid looked as if it had been strained through a burro's bladder.

"You need to be more careful," Slocum said. "Dodge City isn't the kind of place a decent woman walks the streets at night."

"You mean unescorted?"

"I mean at all. The whole Ninth Cavalry wouldn't be enough to protect you from men who haven't seen anything female in six weeks, unless you count a cow or two." He pushed back his plate and got the bill immediately. Slocum glanced at it and saw that it was fair enough. He'd be willing to pay half again what the café owner charged.

That left him enough to get some whiskey, and maybe come back here for breakfast.

"Please, Mr. Slocum, allow me to pay for your meal. It is the least I can do." Ruth reached for the bill. Slocum kept it away from her.

"I pay my own way—no offense. Why don't you get your husband to escort you back to wherever you're staying?"

"I . . . I am not married," she said. Tears formed at the corners of her eyes. "I've come here looking for my father."

Slocum heard the beginning of a long story he wasn't interested in. Bathed, shaved, and fed, he was ready to tie one on.

"I'd be pleased to escort you to your boardinghouse," he said, thinking this would solve his problem and get him into a gambling house the fastest without being rude.

"My father is Phillip Waddell. Perhaps you've heard of him?" Ruth looked at him expectantly.

"Can't say I have, unless he's some relation to No Nose Waddell. Heard tell No Nose lost it in a bar fight." Slocum dropped enough in greenbacks onto the table to satisfy the owner, then offered Ruth his arm.

She accepted.

"Please, sir, don't make fun of me. I have terrible news to relay to my father." She sniffed again and dabbed at her tears with a lace handkerchief. "My mother died two months ago."

"Sorry to hear that, but why'd you come out here to pass along the news?" Slocum asked, in spite of himself. "A telegram is a mite quicker, not to mention cheaper." He looked up and down the street to see if any trouble was brewing.

Slick lay cooling in the still night air. Sometime soon the café owner would complain to the marshal. Not much would come of it since Slick was a drifter, just as Slocum was. Without friends or kin, nobody in Dodge City would much care what happened. Slick's partner groaned and kicked feebly in the dust, still more unconscious than awake. After being buffaloed like he was, the man wasn't likely to come looking for more trouble. He'd figure rightly that he would end up like his partner. A sore head was a country mile better than a bullet in the gut.

"I don't know exactly where my father is, you see," Ruth rattled on. "He came here to take photographs of the West, but he seems to have moved on some weeks ago."

"Too bad. A man ought to know his wife's dead," Slocum said.

"I agree. My father is a great photographer, one of the best," Ruth said. "He worked for Mathew Brady, then for his assistant, Alexander Gardner."

"Heard tell of Brady," Slocum said. He didn't cotton much to men taking pictures of what happened on the battlefield. It was bad enough living through it. To be reminded in a picture years later was a nightmare.

"He's not a nice person," Ruth went on. "He refuses to give individual photographers credit, so my father left and went out on his own. He's had exhibitions in New York and Washington. He's becoming quite prominent as a photographer of the Wild West."

"You've been reading too many penny dreadfuls," Slocum said. "Dodge City isn't the Wild West."

"So father has come to believe," Ruth said. "I need to find him. I do!"

Slocum had walked along, letting the woman lead the way. He wasn't sure where her boardinghouse was, but there had to be onc. Every hotel worth its salt was booked with drovers. The filled feed pens outside town told that more than Bill Granger's herd had arrived recently in Dodge City.

"The National Portrait Gallery," she mused. "That's Mathew Brady's private collection, his museum. It's quite good and has some photographs taken by my father in it."

"Miss Waddell," Slocum said, "I got business to tend to. Sorry that you were upset earlier by those yahoos."

"They won't bother me again," Ruth said, shivering at the thought of Slick lying dead on the boardwalk. "But I was commenting about the portraits because you look familiar. My father tells me I have a good visual memory. Your photograph is in Brady's gallery."

"I doubt it," Slocum said. He had his likeness in other places, notably on wanted posters circulating throughout the West. He had cut down a carpetbagger judge back in Georgia who had needed killing, but the law didn't see it that way.

Time had a way of easing memories—except of judge killers.

"You were in the war. You have that look about you," Ruth said.

"I was in the war. Reckon I might have been shooting at your neighbors."

"It doesn't matter that you fought for the Confederacy," she said firmly.

"I'm glad." Slocum fought to keep the sarcasm from his voice.

"I want to hire you anyway. You are an honorable man. Please find my father so I can tell him about Mama." She turned and looked at Slocum, as if waiting for him to ask how he was to start. This was as far from Slocum's mind as the moon.

"I've got other concerns," Slocum said, taken aback by the young woman's unexpected request.

"I can pay you, Mr. Slocum. Please, this is important and I don't know where to begin." Ruth's words were punctuated by gunfire from the red-light district a few blocks away. Horses galloped hard into the night, and women shrieked curses.

Slocum looked at Ruth and knew she was a fish out of water in Dodge City. That didn't mean he wanted to get mixed up in any wild-goose chase looking for her father. The man might be dead, or he may have decided he liked the fleshy pleasures offered by the Dodge City harlots and was drinking and whoring his way to oblivion. This wouldn't set well with such a refined young lady.

"Fifty dollars," she said, catching him by surprise once more. "I'll give you fifty dollars to make inquiries. He was last seen down by the stockyards. Surely, you can't object to asking a few questions."

"Phillip Waddell?" Slocum scratched his chin. She was offering him as much for a few minutes jawing as he had earned during the past six weeks.

"A photographer," she said, a slight smile coming to her pretty lips. "Please find him for me." Ruth started to fumble in her purse. She pulled out a wad of greenbacks thick enough to choke a cow. Slocum's hand flashed out and covered the roll.

"Don't go showing that where anyone can see it," he said, startled by her naïveté. Even in a city like New York, there had to be footpads willing to cut a friend's throat for a plugged nickel. If there were, Ruth Waddell had never heard of them.

"I forgot," she said. "I do need your help, Mr. Slocum. The last I heard of my father, he was taking photographs of the feed pens and cows coming up from Texas." She gave him the promised fifty dollars.

"How long ago was that?" Slocum asked.

"Almost a month ago. Perhaps only three weeks. The people I queried do not seem to remember the exact date, but it was immediately after the first herd arrived."

"Call it three weeks," Slocum said. Bill Granger's outfit wasn't the first into Dodge, but there hadn't been as many beating him here as there would be coming up the Western Trail in the next month.

"You want it done tonight?" Slocum asked.

"As quickly as possible. I need to speak to him about inheritances, and getting papers signed, and I'd just like to see him again." Ruth's eyes welled with tears once more. Slocum was lost. He had been wavering, in spite of the magnificent sum she offered for asking a few questions.

"What if I can't find out what happened to him? From all you say, he's footloose. He might have decided Denver was a better place to take photographs of beeves." Slocum didn't understand the photographer's fascination with the smelly, ugly longhorns or why anyone would want a picture of one. But then, Slocum didn't understand the likes of Mathew Brady and his war pictures.

"We can discuss this when you find out all that you can of his whereabouts," Ruth said. She paused, smiled shyly and said, "I appreciate this, Mr. Slocum. Really." She stood on tiptoe and gave him a quick kiss on the cheek. She turned and hurried toward her boardinghouse, stopping only when she got to the door to turn and look back.

Slocum tipped his hat in her direction, then damned himself for being such a fool. But the money would ride nicely in his shirt pocket along with his trail wages. He turned and walked the dark streets toward the stockyards. It wouldn't take long to find a yard agent willing to talk about some damn fool Eastern greenhorn setting up complicated gear to take photographs.

Turning into the feedlot he had left only a few hours earlier, he walked between the pens, hunting for someone to question. A single light burned in a small shack to one side. As Slocum approached the shack, he heard loud voices. The lowing cattle drowned out much of what was going on, but the name Waddell drifted to him.

Curious, Slocum went closer. Three men stood outside the door. A tall, thin figure was silhouetted by a lamp inside the shack but Slocum couldn't make out the man's features. And inside another man squealed in pain.

Slocum stood in the shadows and reloaded his six-shooter, not knowing what was going on and not wanting to get involved.

"When?" the tall, thin man demanded. He turned slightly, and Slocum saw a flash of light off military brass. The man wore a ragged Union officer's jacket with its major's clusters tarnished. A saber hung at his left side, and a pistol was jammed into a military holster on his right hip.

"A month back. How the hell should I know?" Again came a loud shriek of pain. Then only the bawling of longhorns filled the stockyard.

The Union officer stepped from the shack. Another man followed him, wiping blood from a knife. In the dim moonlight shining on the yards, the blood looked more like India ink.

"Reckon we won't get more out of him, Major," said the man with the knife.

"A pity." The thin man paced back and forth, his saber clanking. "I want that son of a bitch."

Slocum wasn't sure who the officer meant, but he didn't think it was the dead man inside the shack. The major wouldn't be this agitated since he had obviously given the command to end the other's life.

Slocum moved to go, wondering what he had gotten himself into when he stepped in a mud puddle. The sucking sound was loud enough to be heard over the cattle.

"Stop! I say there, stop! I order you to stop!" The major's voice cracked like a whip.

Slocum turned to face the man, preferring a bullet in the forehead to one in the back.

3

"What are you doing spying on me?" the Union officer asked coldly. He turned so his saber hung back slightly, freeing his hand to go for the pistol in the cavalry holster on his right hip.

Slocum wanted no part of a second gunfight in less than two hours. He didn't know what he'd blundered into here, and he wasn't curious enough to ask.

"I wasn't spying," he said, wondering if the man he faced was able to draw left-handed. That would mean he could get his six-shooter out of the holster as fast as Slocum could draw his Colt Navy. If the major wasn't left-handed, it would be awkward getting a pistol yanked out in time to do anything with its butt stuck backward.

On horseback this would be an asset. Here, now, it would be the major's death, but Slocum wasn't taking any chances. He had a good idea what had gone on inside the tumbledown shack. Somebody lay in a pool of his own blood.

"What are you doing here?" From the way the major shifted his weight, Slocum thought he was left-handed. That made matters a tad more complicated. But not that much.

21

"I was looking for Bill Granger. He owes me money from the drive."

"These aren't Bill Granger's quarters." The major's fingers flexed. He was left-handed. Slocum got ready to see how fast the man was.

"Reckon I was wrong," Slocum said. "Can I buy you gents a drink over at the Lone Star?" He made the offer but knew it would never be accepted.

The major's hand flew toward his right hip and the six-gun holstered there. Slocum had seen faster men, but he couldn't remember when. He went for his own gun, and the world seemed to turn to molasses around him. He saw the major's Colt Army clear leather and start to center on him. Slocum's hand closed on the ebony butt of his six-shooter, but try as he might, he couldn't force any more speed out of his draw.

He was going to die.

There was a puff of white smoke and splinters exploded next to his face. The major's shot had gone wide and had hit a nearby fence. The curious slowness evaporated and then all hell broke loose. Slocum's shot wasn't any better, but it drove the major back into one of his henchmen.

The other man—the one who had been standing watch outside the shack—drew down. Slocum's second shot caught him in the leg and knocked him flat onto his face. Slocum had seen other men do a similar motion when bullets hit solid bone. The man wasn't going to walk away from this.

A hail of lead drove Slocum back.

"Get him, you fool!" the major shouted. "Don't let him go. He must know something."

"He's nothing but a drover," the other man said querulously.

"He's a drover with a six-shooter!"

That argument settled matters for the major's henchman. New waves of death blasted out with foot-long tongues of flame, leaving behind thick and acrid smoke. Slocum ducked down and slid into a pen. The cattle he shared sanctuary with weren't too happy to see him and began pawing the ground. One tried to hook him with a blunted longhorn.

Slocum got to the far side of the feed pen and looked around, trying to figure out the best way to safety. He wasn't going to fight the war all over again, especially since he was outnumbered three to one.

"What the Sam Hill is going on?" came a loud cry. "You stop shootin' in there. This here is the sheriff!"

Slocum used the momentary lull in firing to get farther away. He ducked low when two men rushed past, both carrying sawed-off shotguns.

"Masterson, you get on over there. Catch 'em in a cross fire if they don't give up. We can't have none of these here beeves gettin' shot. There'd be hell to pay for that!"

Slocum saw a well-dressed deputy move toward the shack. The expression on the deputy's face told Slocum that there might be corpses moldering in the dawn light if the major didn't surrender. Seldom had he seen such determination.

"You giving up?" the sheriff called out. "Me and my boys got you surrounded."

"Sheriff, a murder has been committed and you are letting the killer escape." The major stood up with his hands over his head. He had holstered his Colt and was walking forward, boldly telling his lie.

Slocum knew better than to stay now. It would be his word against a cavalry officer's. And the two men with the major weren't inclined to go against their leader's tale, especially the one Slocum had shot in the leg. If the downed man hadn't bled to death, he would walk with a limp the rest of his life.

The cattle protested Slocum's passage through the pens, but he got to the far side of the feedlot without the deputy or sheriff spotting him. He kicked the muck off his boots and pushed his six-shooter back into his holster. The encounter had been brief and in the dark. Slocum didn't think the major could identify him.

And that was fine with him.

Walking back toward Front Street, Slocum had time to put odd pieces together. He was certain he'd heard the major asking after Waddell. But was it Phillip Waddell? Or had Slocum misheard? Ruth hadn't mentioned anyone else hunting for her father. It might be a coincidence.

Slocum didn't believe in coincidence.

He almost returned to Ruth's boardinghouse to tell her of his misadventure and to claim her fifty dollars. Slocum stopped and reconsidered. She didn't seem to be the kind of woman to send him dumb and blind into a shoot-out, and she would have mentioned hiring others to find her father. Slocum wasn't sure a woman like Ruth Waddell would ever run across men like the Union major and his knife-wielding, right-hand man in the course of her day.

Slocum went into the Alhambra and let the smoke and drunken laughter surround him. He ordered a shot of whiskey and was pleased to find it went down smooth as silk. A second shot burned hotly in his gut and let him turn toward the gaming tables. Hawk-eyed men dressed all in black dealt faro.

Slocum's eye was even keener than those playing. The hock and soda cards were fairly handled, but the chips had a way of moving to the house's pile. One dealer clinked through a stack of chips won by a drunk cowboy, counting them twice. The first time was a fair count. The second time, he palmed a chip and slid it back into his own stack.

The cowboy never noticed.

Shrugging this off, Slocum began moving around the room. He wasn't up to playing, even though he knew how the cheating was being done here. It took him ten minutes to find a man slumped in a chair and as parched as the Sonora Desert.

"You got the look of a lonely man," Slocum said. "I'm fresh off the trail and want to buy you a drink."

The man looked apprehensive. "You don't care what I drink? I heard tell how Johnny Ringo done kilt a man for ordering beer when he wanted him drinking whiskey."

"Drink what you like. I need some information, and I'm willing to pay for it." Slocum pulled up a chair. A half bottle of whiskey mysteriously appeared and his greenbacks vanished. He poured two shots; one for himself, and one for his newfound friend.

"Thanks, mister. You're a prince among men," the drunk said, wiping his lips and eyeing the bottle. Slocum pushed it silently toward him. After another drink, he started asking his questions.

"That photograph fella?" the man said, his eyes fogging with liquor. "I remember him from a month back or more— weird cuss, always wantin' to take a picture."

"Know where he is?" asked Slocum.

"What's it to you?" the drunk asked, suddenly more sober. "Seems to be a lot of interest in this fella of late."

"Oh?" Slocum wasn't surprised when he heard the answer.

"That Army fella, the one with the bodyguards all the time trailin' around like he was some foreign p-potentate. He wanted to know about the ph-photographer, too." The man started to hiccup from all the rotgut he had imbibed.

"Do tell," Slocum said, sampling more of the whiskey. This had a bite to it the first drink hadn't possessed. He figured this bottle had been cut with nitric acid to give it the kick of a mule. "And what would this officer's name be?"

"Can't say, but all I can tell you is what I told him. The photographer was askin' all about Denver. How to get there, how long it took, facts he coulda got from any railroad agent."

Slocum pushed the remainder of the bottle over to the grateful man and stood.

"Thanks, mister. You're a darned sight more polite than that Army fella. Wrong side won the war, if you ask me. Too many like him runnin' around makin' life hell for the likes of us."

"Reckon so," Slocum said. He walked from the saloon, and his eyes drifted down the street toward the large jail house. A town like Dodge City needed a calaboose big enough for entire companies of drovers.

Trying to act casual, Slocum worked his way down the crowded street until he came to the jail house. Peering through the dirty window into the sheriff's office, he saw the major and his henchman standing in front a large, battered oak desk.

Slocum turned and looked into the street, his back to the cold brick wall of the sheriff's office. He overheard the conversation inside perfectly.

"Your story is too farfetched to believe, Major Bronston," the sheriff was saying. "You just happened to be walking through the feedlot when you heard old Gus cry out. You moseyed on over and there he was with his throat cut from ear to ear?"

"There is nothing incredible about the truth," the officer said coldly. "Sergeant Dickensen can attest to the accuracy of my statement."

"Can't say I much believe your Sergeant Dickensen, either," the sheriff said. "You just got out of the Detroit Penitentiary. What about him?" The sheriff snorted in disgust.

Deputy Masterson chimed in, "Dickensen's not been lily-white either, Sheriff. I got a telegram from over in Ellsworth that he has a fondness for slicing men up with that Texas toothpick of his."

Slocum frowned. Bronston? Dickensen? The names nudged his memory.

"I served my time," Bronston said. "I discovered a crime in your jurisdiction, attempted to apprehend the miscreant, and now I am being badgered. Is this any way to treat an officer and a gentleman?"

"Officer maybe, but David James Bronston was never a gentleman," Masterson said fiercely. "Sheriff, I say throw the pair of them in jail and wait for Judge Hanks to come along in a day or two. The third one's likely to bleed to death before dawn, but these two we can hang. I think they upped and killed old Gus."

Slocum didn't stay to hear how the argument went. He hoped the young deputy had his way.

He walked up and down the streets, sampling whiskey here and there, listening and asking questions when it wouldn't be too pushy. Slocum didn't like the way the scant details he discovered fell into a pile.

Major Bronston had spent a good deal of time threatening and blowing hard to get information about Phillip Waddell. If Slocum believed half of the stories about the Union major, he was the bloodiest butcher since Slocum's former commanding officer, William Quantrill.

Slocum didn't know what he was going to tell Ruth Waddell about her father. The photographer was long gone from Dodge City. That he had someone like Bronston hot on his heels didn't bode well for the man. But what would stir up Bronston so much that he was willing to kill to find out the photographer's whereabouts?

The more people Slocum asked about Waddell, the murkier the picture got. The man seemed harmless. If anything, most of the locals thought he was nothing more than a crackpot.

Bellied up to the Lone Star Saloon's long bar, Slocum motioned the barkeep for another shot. He was feeling mellow and was at the point of making a decision about what to tell Ruth Waddell.

"You remember a photographer in here a few weeks back?" Slocum asked the barkeep.

The man's long walrus mustache twitched as he broke into a crooked smile.

"I remember him. You a friend?"

"Can't say that I am but—"

The expression on the bartender's face caused Slocum to bite off his explanation. He moved slightly to get the thong off his six-shooter. Turning a little to his left, Slocum looked behind him.

The deputy stood in the door and his gaze fixed Slocum square in his place as surely as if he had used a knife.

"You, the one at the bar," Masterson said. "I want a word with you."

Slocum got ready to shoot his way out of town.

4

"What can I do for you, Deputy?" Slocum asked, keeping his voice level. His heart started to pound. He didn't want to gun down the deputy sheriff. From what little he had seen of Masterson, he liked the young man. This wouldn't stop Slocum from killing him, though, if it came to that.

"You came in with Bill Granger's crew, didn't you?"

Slocum cursed himself for mentioning Granger when Major Bronston had braced him outside the shack in the feedlot. This was the only way the deputy could have known he'd ridden with the Texas rancher.

"Reckon so. Bill Granger's a good man to work for. Is there something wrong?"

"A man's been killed," Masterson said. Slocum recognized the trick. If he so much as hinted that he knew what had gone on in Gus's run-down shack, he'd be looking at the world from the wrong side of Dodge City's jail house bars.

"Not Bill? Don't remember him so much as tasting whiskey. Or was it Rusty Neal? He's got a hot head and a fast hand when the mood's on him."

Slocum saw that his feigned ignorance was working. Masterson didn't know who he was talking about when he mentioned Neal.

"We got word you were seen out in the feedlot tonight. You wanted to see Granger about wages he owed you."

Slocum moved slowly as he went to his shirt pocket. He pulled out his six weeks' worth of pay and showed it to the deputy. "He paid me with the rest of the drovers around sundown. We're square."

"I know your face," Masterson said. "You been in Dodge City before?"

"Drifted through now and then, but I never stayed longer than I plan to this time," Slocum said honestly. "I'm figuring on having another drink or two, in which you are welcome to join me, then I'm going to find a place to sleep and be on my way in the morning."

"Where you heading?" Masterson was a curious lawman. Slocum hated them worst of all. They never stopped asking until they prodded a man into action, either running or fighting.

"Don't rightly know. Maybe back down into Texas, though I haven't seen Denver in a spell. Whichever way my horse's face turns come dawn tomorrow is the direction I'll be going."

Slocum saw the deputy's indecision. Bronston must have spun quite a tale to get the lawman to scour every saloon in town for the cowboys who had worked their way north with Bill Granger's herd. Masterson gave him the once-over a final time, and then turned his attention to the others in the saloon. Slocum didn't relax until the deputy left.

"Wonder what that was all about?" the barkeep asked. "He said somebody'd been killed but never said who it was."

Slocum shrugged. He'd meant every word he had just

spoken. There wasn't anything holding him in Dodge City past tomorrow morning.

Then the barkeep got a bad case of remembering.

"You were asking after that photographer named Waddell, weren't you?" The barkeep twirled his thick mustache and looked thoughtful. "He wanted to capture old Iron Foot's image with that camera box of his. Waddell might have said something to the old Injun 'bout his traveling plans."

"Iron Foot?" Slocum was drawn in despite what he had intended.

"A Cherokee what lives outside of town a mile or two. Out east of town, near the old lightning-struck tree. Snuck off the reservation down in Indian Territory a couple times. He's a harmless old galoot."

"Think this Iron Foot knows about Waddell's whereabouts?"

"Might," the barkeep said, polishing shot glasses and rearranging the dirt on them. "Heard tell he spent damned near a week with the Injun. Can't imagine anyone spendin' that much time with Iron Foot."

Slocum drank slowly, considering what he ought to do. Finding Waddell looked to be a task that could get himself killed. Major Bronston and his henchmen weren't too sociable and looked to be the kind to murder anyone in their path. But Slocum was beginning to wonder what the hell was going on. Ruth Waddell seemed an innocent enough young woman in her desire to find her father. Slocum came to a quick decision, finished his whiskey, and left the saloon.

He stopped at the livery stable for his mare. The tow-headed boy rubbed sleep from his eyes as he brought the horse out for Slocum.

"I'm looking for a Cherokee who goes by the name of Iron Foot. You know where I can find him?"

"Iron Foot? That old blowhard?" The boy laughed. "If he owes you money, you're fresh out of luck, mister."

"Let's say I want to talk to him," Slocum said carefully. He was getting spooked every time he heard a horse or gunfire along Dodge City's streets. The coldness in Bronston's face and the stark blood lust in the one the sheriff called Sergeant Dickensen added some urgency to finding the Indian and Phillip Waddell.

The boy gave the directions, and Slocum rode at a quick trot. The horse complained a mite but was up to the demands Slocum placed on her. It was almost two in the morning when Slocum reined back, and saw the sod house built against the lee side of a rise near a tree burned and broken from a lightning bolt. A thin column of smoke rose from a hole in the roof, showing someone lived there.

Slocum dismounted, tethered his horse, and approached on foot. He froze when he heard a low chuckle.

"You move good. Almost Cherokee good."

"Iron Foot?"

"You know me?" The voice came from the side of the sod house. Slocum's eyes probed the shadows until he found a spot darker than the surroundings.

"I'm looking for Phillip Waddell. Heard tell you and him got to be friends a few weeks ago."

"Ah, the man with the magic box." The Indian hobbled into view. Slocum blinked. He didn't know what he had expected but this wasn't it. Iron Foot had to be seventy years old if he was a day. Age had bent him slightly, but there was no hint of dullness in his sharp, darting eyes. A knife hung at his side, and his buckskins made a soft hissing noise as he moved.

"Others are looking for him. I'm afraid they want to harm him."

"Phillip Waddell? He has enemies of such strength?" Iron

Foot hobbled over and put his back to the sod wall, then slid down. He crossed his legs, and Slocum thought he had gone to sleep.

After several minutes, Iron Foot looked up, motioned for Slocum to sit beside him, and then held out a small silver flask filled with whiskey.

"Phillip Waddell gave this to me. I let him capture my image for his speaking leaves. . . ."

"Book?" asked Slocum, taking the whiskey. To his surprise, it was good quality. He took enough to be polite and handed it back.

"He makes many speaking leaves and puts with them his photographs. He took my picture and listened to my story. He is a good man."

Again Iron Foot fell silent. Slocum waited, knowing the Cherokee was considering if he ought to tell Slocum anything. Almost five minutes later, Iron Foot spoke.

"You are from my home. I can tell by your voice."

"Georgia?"

"I was born just after Whitepath led the rebellion." Iron Foot sighed. "He was a dreamer. He thought we could fight the white eyes and win. It was like pushing back a river with one hand. We got wet, and we failed."

"You lived along the Chestatee River?" Slocum had heard stories of the Cherokees who had lived along the river before gold was discovered in Ward's Creek in July, 1829. His father had told him how John Ross had fought all the way to the Supreme Court and won, only to have Andy Jackson tell John Marshall to enforce his own court orders against evicting the Cherokee.

The Cherokees had been forcibly moved in 1835, after a long battle.

"Whitepath was a dreamer," Iron Foot said. "He could not see what others did."

Slocum did not comment. If Iron Foot wanted to tell him about Waddell, he would in his own time.

"Phillip Waddell mentioned a daughter. You work for her?"

"Ruth Waddell has come from New York with sad news. Waddell's wife has died." Slocum accepted the silver flask again.

"Phillip Waddell took my picture and put my words down on the speaking leaves. He believed I was once a mighty warrior. He spoke of his daughter." Iron Foot took a long pull, then tucked his flask away. "What is it you want to know?"

"I've heard he planned to go to Denver. If so, his daughter needs to go there to find him."

"Denver, yes," Iron Foot said, "but that is only a place to rest along the longer path. He goes to what he called Devils Tower. I have heard Arapaho speak of it, but they are such liars. Who can believe them?"

Slocum frowned at this. He had heard of Devils Tower up in Wyoming, but he didn't know what drew Waddell there. Then again, Slocum wasn't sure what the photographer's motives were in coming West to take his pictures.

"Thank you, Iron Foot," Slocum said. He rose to leave.

"A moment," the Cherokee called. "What of these others who seek Phillip Waddell?"

"One wears a Union major's jacket and carries a cavalry saber."

"So many bluecoats," Iron Foot said, shrugging. "They would harm Phillip Waddell?"

"I don't know what they want, but from the bodies they're leaving behind, that might be true." Slocum waited but Iron Foot said nothing more. He walked away slowly, mounted, and rode back into Dodge City. A few minutes before dawn he reined back in front of the boardinghouse where Ruth Waddell was staying.

It was a bit early but Slocum needed to pass along what he had learned. Although it hadn't been a promise, he had told Deputy Masterson he was leaving town, and Slocum had every intention of doing so.

He stopped in the middle of the walk when he heard a window being pulled open. He looked up and saw Ruth motioning to him. She was still in her white, frilly nightgown.

"Mr. Slocum, please be quiet. The others aren't up yet. I'll let you in and—"

"Never mind," Slocum said. He went to the trellis under Ruth's window and caught hold of the vines. It took only a few seconds for him to come even with her windowsill. "Your father's gone to Denver on his way up into Wyoming, to a place called Devils Tower. I—"

"Please, come inside." Ruth stepped back. For a moment, Slocum hesitated. The lamp beside her bed cast enough light to silhouette her slim body through the thin nightgown.

"This isn't proper," Slocum said.

"Don't worry. I need to know what you have learned." Ruth sat on the bed as Slocum scrambled into the room. He looked around for a chair, but he didn't see one in the small room. Ruth patted the bed beside her. He sat down gingerly. Ruth Waddell was a well-bred Eastern woman of obvious education. It wouldn't do her reputation any good being found with a drover in her room.

"Your father spent a considerable time with a Cherokee outside town. They got to be friends." Slocum went on to tell her all Iron Foot had related to him.

"Father wanted only unique images of the West. From what you tell me of this Devils Tower, it is precisely the sort of photograph he would insist on including in his book."

She tossed her long chestnut hair back to get it away from her eyes.

Slocum's heart almost skipped a beat. She was about the most beautiful woman he had ever seen—and this wasn't six weeks on the trail talking.

"We need to hurry after him to—"

"We?" Slocum interrupted. "I found out what you needed to know. That's all I intend doing." He hesitated telling her about Bronston and Dickensen, yet she needed to know. He started to, but she cut him off before he could say a word.

"Mr. Slocum!" she protested. Softer, she said, "John, please, you're a gentleman. You must help. I simply cannot continue on to Denver by myself. I need someone to ask questions and get answers, and you know I would never be able to."

"This isn't what I had in mind doing after a trail drive."

"If it's money, I'll pay you more. A hundred dollars to see me to Denver and another hundred to find Father at this Devils Tower." She moved closer. Her brown eyes glowed. Slocum got uncomfortable at the thoughts running through his mind. She kept telling him what a Southern gentleman he was, and what he was beginning to feel wasn't very gentlemanly.

"It's not that—" He never got any farther. She moved still closer and kissed him square on the lips.

She broke off and said in a husky whisper, "You're so different from other men. So polite, so strong."

"This isn't right," Slocum said. He tried to stand.

"Wait, John, don't go. I want you now." Ruth's voice almost broke with strain. "Please stay, just a while. It doesn't matter if you come with me or not. But stay. Stay." She reached out and unbuckled his gun belt. Then she started working on the buttons on his shirt.

Her long fingers stroked over his chest, stirring deep

emotions inside him. When she moved lower and pressed into the mound at the crotch of his jeans, Slocum thought he was going to explode.

"Ruth," he said, "you don't have to do this."

"I want to," she insisted. Now the brunette's lips crushed with real desire against Slocum's. She pressed him back to the bed and Slocum knew he was lost. Ruth might not be doing this to bind him to her hunt for Phillip Waddell, but it was working that way.

He kicked his jeans off while she lifted her nightgown. For a moment Slocum could only stare. He knew she was beautiful, but he hadn't expected such alabaster perfection. Reaching out, he took her breasts in his hands and stroked the silken flesh.

Ruth closed her eyes and shivered with delight. She moved forward slightly, crushing her breasts harder into the palms of his hands. Slocum felt her nipples begin to harden with desire. Ruth began moaning softly and rubbing herself up and down against him like a contented cat.

"I want more, John. I *need* more." She gripped his iron-hard length and began tugging insistently on it. He wasn't able to put up with this for long.

He let her guide him to the warm, moist spot nestled between her thighs. Slocum rolled over on top of her, poised to enter.

Looking down into her chocolate-colored eyes he saw the answer to his unspoken question. He still hesitated, not sure she understood what she was asking from him. In those eyes he saw not a young girl but a mature woman—and she wanted what he had to offer.

Hips levering forward slowly, he entered her. A soft shudder passed through Ruth's body. The brunette tossed her head from side to side, sending a halo of fragrant hair over the white linen pillowcase. When he was buried balls-deep in her, Slocum paused to allow the sensations to ripple through him.

Keeping still for long wasn't possible. She gripped down around his length with hidden muscles, squeezing, teasing, and goading him to action. He withdrew and then slid forward faster. He repeated this, picking up speed until he found the rhythm that gave them both the maximum pleasure.

"Yes, John, you fill me up so much! More, give me more!" she sobbed out. Her fingers clawed along his upper arms and his back, leaving tiny scratches. He hardly noticed.

He was lost in the world of his own passion. The fiery tide mounting in his loins threatened to spill forth at any instant. Slocum tried to hold it back to give—and get— even more pleasure, but everything the woman did robbed him of his control.

She bucked up with her hips grinding hard. Her fingers stroked and clawed, soothed and stimulated. Her firm breasts began to flush with color, which quickly spread up to her shoulders and neck. Slocum watched in fascination and then he had his hands full with a wildcat.

Ruth Waddell shrieked, moaned, and ground herself hard against him, trying to get as much of his manhood into her body as possible. She reached around and grabbed his ass, pulling him in powerfully. Slocum tried to oblige but the movement caused him to gasp and thrust one more time, as though he was trying to split her apart.

He shuddered as he spilled his seed, then sank down on top of her. Ruth smiled in contentment with her eyelids half closed.

She had said this wouldn't bind him if he wanted to go. Slocum knew exactly what she had done. He was as bound to her now as if she had forged steel around his wrists and heart.

5

Slocum lay alongside the beautiful woman in the narrow feather bed listening to her soft breathing. He stared at the boardinghouse's cracked plaster ceiling and wondered what he ought to do.

He slipped from Ruth Waddell's bed and stood, staring at her peaceful form. She had said she wanted him, no strings attached. For Slocum it wasn't quite that easy, and he didn't have to wake her up to know it wasn't for her, either. But her road was different from his. Slocum had enjoyed making love with her, but it had to end here and now. Ruth Waddell wasn't his kind of woman.

Dressing quietly, he went to the window and looked out into the street. Dodge City was coming alive; the working people were on their way to stores and gainful employment. The cowboys who had been hooting and hollering all night would be sleeping off too much whiskey or bemoaning their hangovers—some of them in the town jail.

Slocum started out the window, then paused. He might be seen. Whatever had happened between him and Ruth ought to stay private. It wouldn't do if he tarnished her reputation, even if she was going to take the next train to Denver. Instead of climbing back down the trellis, Slocum went to the door, feeling his way as if there were loose boards in the floor.

He paused, and looked back at her lovely face. He saw the rise and fall of her naked breasts, and longed again for the touch of her hand on his body. Then he left quickly. Slocum knew he couldn't think about the brunette too much or he would be wrapped up in a cocoon stronger than any prison.

The owner of the boardinghouse was just coming from her room. Slocum ducked down the rear stairs and got out the back door before anyone saw him. He sucked in the tepid morning air, then he stretched, and wondered where he would go. He had the money from the drive in his pocket. Ruth had promised him fifty dollars, but he had never collected it. And right now, he considered himself well enough paid for his trouble.

He went around to the front, got his horse, and walked it toward the stable. The towheaded boy rubbed his eyes sleepily when he saw Slocum.

"You back, mister? I figured you would still be riding."

"Curry my horse, give her a bag of grain, and get her ready for the trail by eight." He fumbled out a two bit piece and tossed it to the boy, who snagged the spinning coin with the ease of long practice.

"She'll be rarin' to go when you get back," the blond boy promised.

Slocum went to find breakfast. His belly was rubbing up against his backbone, and he needed another thick steak to put things right. As he walked along Front Street he had the eerie sensation he was walking through a ghost town.

He stopped and looked around. The bustle from the night before was over, but there was something else haunting him. Slocum tried to find even one person out on the street. Nobody was in sight. He turned slowly, his sharp eyes looking for signs of life. He heard more than he saw.

Dodge City seemed to have turned into a den of timid mice scurrying in their holes to escape a coyote.

Slocum had seen similar occurrences, and it chilled him. Something big was going to happen, and no one wanted to be outside and an easy target when the shooting started. He ducked into a saloon without even bothering to see which one it was.

A bartender looked up with fear blazing brightly in his eyes. He let out a tiny yelp and vanished into the back room. Slocum heard a heavy bar drop into place. Getting the barkeep out would take a battering ram. This only made Slocum more curious.

"What the hell's going on?" he shouted to the hidden barkeep. Slocum heard wood squeaking and then a heavy slamming. He puzzled it out; the barkeep must have opened a trapdoor, then dropped through it into the cellar. In this neck of the woods, such hidey-holes were reserved for hiding from tornadoes.

Slocum went back outside and peered up at the sky, hunting for a twister. They called this Tornado Alley, and with good reason. But the sky wasn't the typical ominous corroded copper-green, and none of the slow-moving clouds showed the spiral motion hinting that there was a tornado ready to drop down and rape the town.

Going to the bar, Slocum leaned over, grabbed a bottle, and poured himself a drink. He drank quickly. The trade whiskey burned his throat and tore at his gut, but it chased away some of the gnawing hunger he felt.

Time to move out, he decided. A second drink on the house went down smoother than the first. Slocum started to replace the bottle, but then decided to take it with him. The barkeep hadn't been too hospitable, and the gift of the bottle would go a ways to setting things right.

Slocum stepped out into the street just as a bullet sang through the air. The bottle exploded in his hand and showered him with whiskey and broken glass.

Before the neck of the broken bottle hit the boardwalk, Slocum's hand had dragged out his Colt Navy, but there was no one in sight. Slocum ducked down and jumped off the walk, taking refuge at the side of the saloon. He couldn't see who had shot at him.

The sheriff's voice echoed from down the street. "Give it up, Slocum. We got you dead to rights."

"What's going on, Sheriff?" Slocum shifted his position to get a better shot at him should he be foolish enough to show himself. The sheriff had been in Dodge City long enough to know better. He stayed hidden and kept Slocum guessing as to his whereabouts.

"We got an arrest warrant on you, Slocum. Judge killing ain't good, no matter where you did it."

"Who told you that, Sheriff? He's a damned liar!" Slocum looked around for some way to escape. He was only playing for time because the charge was true.

Slocum had ridden with Quantrill's Raiders and had been gut-shot by Bloody Bill Anderson when he complained about the Lawrence, Kansas, massacre of women and children. It had taken months for him to recover, and when he had gone home to the Slocum farm in Calhoun, Georgia, he found his family dead. They were dead, and a carpetbagger judge was eyeing the land for use as a stud farm. Charges were made of not paying taxes during the war, and Slocum couldn't come close to paying the extortionate rates that were being demanded. One night, the judge and a hired gun rode up to the Slocum farm. Only John Slocum rode out that night. Up near the springhouse, two fresh graves remained. Slocum had been on the run ever since.

"Deputy Masterson's got a good memory. He saw a poster on you that floated past a year back."

Slocum figured as much. Slocum was sure he and Masterson had never crossed paths before, and this eliminated most of the reasons for the look of almost recognition on the man's face. Masterson had seen the poster and commented on it.

"You got the wrong man, Sheriff," Slocum said, crouching down and looking for a way out. Crossing the street was foolhardy. He'd get cut down before he reached the far side. That left only one direction.

He turned and looked down the alley and saw two six-shooters leveled at him. Behind one Dickensen sneered, and behind the other, Bronston's grin was pure evil. The major lifted his pistol, sighted, and squeezed off a round.

Slocum dived out into the street, in spite of the sheriff waiting for him. Bullets danced in the dirt from Bronston, Dickensen, and from the sheriff down the street. Slocum rolled, then stopped, and kicked back hard in the opposite direction. He had seen jackrabbits dance around like this trying to avoid a hunter's rifle.

Now he knew how the rabbit felt.

Slocum didn't even bother using his own Colt. There wasn't a good target. Ducking and darting back and forth was the only way he was likely to keep alive.

He would have died if lady luck hadn't smiled on him, however briefly. A wagon rumbled down the street, its driver oblivious to the gunfire. Slocum rolled across the thoroughfare, feeling a hot streak cross his back. The lead had almost cut him in two, but the wagon rumbled on and gave Slocum his chance.

Staying down, he fought to get under the wagon's wheels and grab the undercarriage. Chains dangled, and the axles grated and moaned with the weight of the load in the bed. Greasy links slipped through his fingers, but Slocum succeeded in catching the rear axle. He pulled hard and got his body up as far as he could, but his heels still dragged in the dusty street.

"Where'd he get off to?" called the sheriff. Slocum rumbled past, catching sight of the lawman's legs and nothing more. From down the street came angry shouts as Bronston and Dickensen followed him. They had no problem with firing at the wagon and its driver because it was the only way they could stop Slocum from getting away.

Splinters exploded all around him. Slocum was well enough protected, but the driver wasn't. The driver let out a bellow of rage and spun around, aware of what was going on around him for the first time. Through cracks in the wagon's frame Slocum saw the man yank out a sawed-off shotgun. The dual roars as he pumped buckshot back in Bronston's direction were music to Slocum's ears.

A small war had started. The sheriff thought Bronston and Dickensen were firing at him—and the wagon driver was definitely firing at the two Union soldiers. Lead sang along Front Street until Slocum worried that the wagon might be reduced to rubble around him. But the driver had no intention of standing and fighting it out with the bushwhackers behind him. He reloaded and fired twice more, then used the reins to urge his two mules to more speed. Slocum was caught unawares and lost his grip. He fell into the street and had to scramble to keep from being run over by the back wheels. He lay in the dust for a moment until he got his breath back, then got his feet under him, and raced for an alley so he could get his bearings.

Gunshots from back down the street told him that his antagonists were no longer shooting at him. Bronston and the sheriff were now exchanging rounds, each mistaking the other as the enemy. Slocum wasn't going to correct either side. Both deserved shallow graves out in the town's potter's field. Staying alive held more interest for him than a peaceful Dodge City.

Slocum looked around and didn't like what he saw. He was too far from the stables to get back easily. Without his horse, he was a sitting duck.

He crouched down and checked his Colt Navy, making sure it carried six rounds in its cylinder. Thinking hard, he decided the sheriff was nobody's fool. If Masterson knew of the wanted poster, and the deputy wasn't with the sheriff, that meant he was watching the stable. Going there would be the same as sticking his foot into a bear trap.

"My horse," Slocum grumbled. "It's hard finding ponies as good as that one." But if it came to leaving the horse behind and escaping, or trying to get it and dying, he knew which he'd choose.

Slocum considered finding Bill Granger and pleading with him for help. He shook off any such notion. Granger was a good man, loyal to a fault, but he wouldn't want to come between the law and a judge killer. If anything, Bill Granger was a bit too upright in his dealings. He'd never be able to figure out how killing a judge could be proper.

He thought of the others who had ridden side by side with him over the past six weeks. Rusty Neal might be willing to help. He had hinted that he had trouble with the law down in Texas and wasn't kindly disposed toward the lawmen in Dodge City, but Slocum had no idea where to find him— or the others he'd ridden with.

"Ruth," he said aloud. He had walked out on her and hadn't intended on returning, but she seemed his only chance now. If she could get his mare from the stables, she might be able to bring her to him. Then he could get the hell away from a lawman obsessed with crimes from years past rather than maintaining the current peace.

Slocum used back streets and pressed close to the walls of buildings as he made his way toward the boardinghouse where he had left Ruth Waddell only an hour earlier. He slowed and studied the place. It seemed quiet enough, but he was growing wary. Walking into a trap was the last thing he wanted to do.

He started across the street to the boardinghouse when his sixth sense warned him of trouble. Slocum didn't know if anyone associated him with the woman, but the evidence was there. He had been asking after Phillip Waddell, and Ruth had made no secret of her identity. If anything, she might have raised up enough dust on her own, looking for her father, to connect her with Slocum.

Looking straight ahead, Slocum hurried past the boardinghouse. Only when he reached the general store did he slow down. He went to the pickle barrel on the walk, and peered down into it as if choosing carefully. He used this as a cover to study the street behind him.

Two men lounged in front of a bakery, eating fresh bread. The glint of sunlight off one of their badges warned Slocum that he had been lucky again. If they hadn't gotten hungry and gone into the bakery, they would have spotted him for sure. He heaved a sigh, went into the general store, and walked straight for the back door.

The proprietor never saw him, he was working under a counter. Slocum ducked into the alley behind the store, dashed across the open space, and came up behind the boardinghouse. A woman was hanging out wash on a long line—the same woman Slocum had almost been seen by earlier.

She looked up. Slocum tipped his hat and greeted her.

"Morning, ma'am. I'm looking for Miss Waddell. Is this where she's lodging?"

"Used to be," the woman said, paying more attention to fastening the laundry to the line than to Slocum. "She left not more'n fifteen minutes ago. Said she was going to. . . ." The woman stopped and stared hard at Slocum for the first time. "What's it to you?"

"I was doing some work for her and forgot to deliver part of it. She was on her way to Denver. Is she at the train station?" Slocum saw from the woman's expression he had hit the nail on the head. "Much obliged, and sorry to trouble you like this."

The boardinghouse's owner sniffed and dug down into her laundry basket for more wet wash. In the hot Kansas sun it would be dry in nothing flat. Then she could get on to fixing lunch for her paying boarders.

Slocum was faced with the same problem he had before. Masterson would be watching the stable. But how many men would be examining every passenger at the railroad station? Maybe not many. What cowboy was willing to leave a town without his horse?

Counting on this bit of misjudgment, Slocum turned and ran toward the depot. He heard a long, loud whistle signaling that the train was coming into the station. This gave more speed to his boots. He got to the platform as the last of the passengers were boarding.

"Is this the train for Denver?" he asked the ticket agent. The bored man never looked up from his newspaper.

"Reckon it is. See the side of the train?"

"It says Denver and Rio Grande."

"You can read. Good. It's a useful skill. You wanting a ticket or not? Better hurry 'cuz it's about due to pull out."

Slocum started to get money from his shirt pocket for the ticket when he saw movement out of the corner of his eye.

The law hadn't thought of the railroad station, but Major Bronston had.

Sunlight glinted off his cavalry saber as he marched onto the platform. Beside him, strutting along like a sergeant major, was Dickensen and behind them came two more men. All had a distinct military bearing, in spite of the lack of real uniforms.

Even if Bronston was no longer a major, he carried his rank with him, and he barked out commands as if he headed a column of cavalry a mile long.

"There he is! Get him!"

Slocum didn't wait to catch a round in his belly. He ran for the far end of the platform. Bullets started singing around him as he dived off the platform and swung around to face them. The two men with Bronston and Dickensen were making a frontal assault.

Slocum showed them the folly of such an attack. He cut them down just as his brother and too many other good men had been slaughtered at Pickett's Charge. He squeezed off one round that caught one of the men high in the chest. His second bullet found a target in the other's gut. Slocum tried to finish him off; being gut shot was worse than outright dying, but Dickensen and Bronston entered the fight and prevented him from making a killing shot.

The train creaked and groaned as it started to move, and hot steam blasted from its pistons. The powerful engine began pulling harder and harder, and the train slowly left the station. Slocum judged his chances for getting on board and deemed them good.

He shoved his six-shooter back into his cross-draw holster and bolted for the train. He immediately found Bronston and Dickensen waiting for such a move.

Both men opened up, driving him back for shelter.

The train's whistle let out a mournful cry and the caboose clanked on by. Slocum had missed his chance for getting aboard, and down the street leading to the depot he saw the sheriff and two deputies riding up, all primed to capture their judge killer.

6

Slocum dived under the station's rickety wood platform and scooted as fast as he could. He kicked up enough dirt to cover him, but he was past caring. If he didn't get out of the cross fire between Bronston and the sheriff, he was a goner. He angled across from where he had gone under the platform and came out near the front of the station. Peering between uneven boards, he saw the sheriff and a deputy he didn't recognize jump off their horses. Boots clattered over his head as they raced into the station.

To hesitate now was to be lost forever. Slocum could feel the hemp noose tightening around his neck. He kicked hard and knocked loose a board. He squeezed between two others and came out in front of the station. The sheriff's horse reared as Slocum slipped its reins into his hand.

"There, there, old paint," he said, trying to soothe the animal. Slocum vaulted into the saddle and put his heels to the animal's flanks. The horse tried to buck, but Slocum kept his seat. He had ridden worse sunfishers than this in his day.

The horse neighed in protest, but as soon as he saw that Slocum was bound and determined to stay in his seat, he gave up and galloped off obediently.

Slocum heard shouts behind him, but he kept low. He knew the sheriff would never rest until he tracked down a judge killer and a horse thief, especially when it was his horse that had been stolen.

He could never hope to outrun a posse, but if luck still rode with him, Slocum knew he wouldn't have to. He guided the horse to a path alongside the railroad tracks. In the distance the train let loose a high plume of steam and a mournful whistle as it rounded a curve and turned toward Denver. He had to catch up before the long train got up to full speed. Even the fastest horse would never be able to catch the Denver & Rio Grande engine on a level run.

Slocum bent low and felt the hot, humid Kansas wind whip past his face. He squinted and saw he was narrowing the gap between himself and the train—but the horse was tiring rapidly. It had galloped full out for almost a half mile. Any more and it might collapse in exhaustion beneath him.

Slocum whipped the horse to keep it running.

The lathered horse was snorting foam now and beginning to falter. A missed step would send Slocum hurtling to the ground and he would certainly be captured.

"Keep going, damn you, keep going!" Slocum urged.

And the horse did. A burst of speed put Slocum's fingers within inches of the railing on the caboose, but as sudden as the burst of speed had come—it died. Slocum had to decide.

He got his feet out of the stirrups and managed to kick off, using the saddle to brace himself for a split second. He sailed through the air as the horse faltered and broke stride. His strong fingers closed on the rusty railing.

Slocum found himself being dragged along behind the train. He shouted, heaved, and got himself up and over the iron railing with scant damage done to his legs or arms. Dusting himself off, he peered inside the caboose. The conductor and a mail clerk were playing gin. Slocum decided not to bother them. He went up the outer ladder and got onto the roof of the caboose. Walking gingerly, he made his way forward until he came to the last passenger car. He dropped to the platform between cars, and dusted himself off.

A few live sparks from the smokestack had caught on his clothing and threatened to burn holes. When he had cleaned off the sparks and soot as best as he could, he went into the car and looked around.

The passengers were trying to doze or were just staring out the window at the slow progress the train made in leaving Kansas and getting to Colorado. But nowhere among them did he see Ruth Waddell. Slocum wobbled and rolled with the motion of the train as he made his way forward out of the car. When he got to the next car, he rubbed dirt off the window and looked into it. A smile crossed his face.

Slocum made his way along the aisle and slid into the seat across from Ruth. The woman was reading a book and didn't look up, even though a sour expression crossed her face. She had hoped to have both seats to herself on the trip.

Slocum cleared his throat, but Ruth continued to ignore him.

"If the job is still open, I wouldn't mind taking it," he finally said. The brunette jumped as if someone had poked her with a firebrand. Her eyes widened and her mouth tried to form words. For all the world, she looked like a fish flopped up on a beach and struggling to breathe.

"John!" she finally blurted. "I never expected to see you again. Why? What?" She couldn't get the words to come out right. Flustered, she finally lapsed into silence.

"I got to figuring that finding your father was more important than anything else I had to do," he said. "If you're still willing to pay the two hundred dollars, I reckon I can see fit to devote a week or two to the pursuit."

"I'll do better than that," she said with fire in her eyes. "I'll pay five hundred dollars!"

"You don't have to go that high," Slocum said, fighting his natural inclination to see what sum the lovely woman would settle on.

"What changed your mind?" she asked. He started to speak but she cut him off. "Really."

Her innocence and openness got to him. He had a lie all ready for the telling, but he couldn't bring himself to use it now. Ruth Waddell wanted honesty and she deserved it.

"I got into a bit of trouble in Dodge City," he said honestly. "Most of it had nothing to do with hunting for your father, but some of it did."

"Whatever do you mean?" Ruth closed her book and sat primly with her hands folded in her lap.

"There's a Union major who's hot to find your father. He's got several men with him, all with the look of Yankee regulars about them. Do you know a Major Bronston?" He watched her expression and saw only puzzlement. Ruth had either never heard of the man, or was a better actress than he gave her credit for being.

"What does this Bronston have to do with Father?"

"Do you know a Sergeant Dickensen? He's Bronston's right-hand man."

"To the best of my knowledge I have never heard of either man. Can you describe them? Perhaps they are friends of Father's who I never met formally."

Slocum doubted they were Phillip Waddell's friends. Bronston had blood in his eye, for whatever reason, and Dickensen was the kind to kill his own grandmother if a superior officer ordered it. Slocum had seen men like Dickensen throughout the war and hated every mother's son of their murderous rank. He had also seen men like Bronston and gotten more than his fill of them, too. They were the kind who took Sherman's orders to heart as they marched through Georgia. They were the men who rode with Quantrill. They were guilty of the worst crimes possible, and all done in the name of the Union or the Confederacy.

Slocum described the tall, thin, left-handed Bronston for Ruth, but she shook her head. "He does not seem familiar. He might be a friend of Mathew Brady's. So many men came through the studios when Father worked for Mr. Brady that I never could keep them straight."

"If you saw Bronston, you wouldn't forget him," Slocum assured her. He was sure he'd never forget the feral gleam in the man's eye or the expression on Bronston's face when he had ordered his sergeant to kill some innocent fool back at the stockyards.

"What does this Major Bronston have to do with Father going to Devils Tower?"

"I don't know. Maybe nothing. Maybe Bronston doesn't care where he finds your father, but if I'm any judge, he means serious harm."

"He would *kill* Father?" Ruth Waddell was aghast at the notion of one man harming another.

Before Slocum could speak, the conductor made his way down the aisle, punching tickets. Slocum leaned back, not wanting to talk in front of the man. A telegram might be sent along the line asking that anyone matching Slocum's description be stopped. If the conductor paid him no attention, he might not remember him later if a wire did come in.

"Ticket," the conductor said, staring at Ruth Waddell. She smiled prettily and handed him her ticket.

Before the conductor could turn to him, Slocum said in a low voice, "I need some of that money to pay for the ticket, Miss Waddell." Slocum hated using Ruth's name like this, but it kept the conductor's attention focused on her.

"You paying for his ticket, Miss Waddell?" The conductor let her name roll off his tongue as if it were honeyed wine. Slocum had counted on the man's interest being in the brunette's beauty and not in some drover accompanying her.

"Certainly, sir. Here." Ruth fumbled out a few greenbacks and gave them to the conductor. He stuffed them into his coat pocket. Slocum wondered if the railroad would ever see a penny of that money. Somehow, he doubted it.

"If there's anything I can do to be of service, Miss Waddell, just ask for me." The conductor went on, whistling off-key. It was seldom he had passengers of such surpassing beauty.

Slocum thanked her and leaned back, tipping his hat down over his eyes. He hadn't gotten much sleep the night before, but he wasn't complaining. By taking this job he might be able to spend a few more nights as pleasurably, and he was certainly beyond the reach of the Dodge City sheriff and Major Bronston for the time being. Slocum drifted off to a fitful sleep, rocked and tossed by the rolling train motion.

"This is a much larger city than I anticipated," Ruth Waddell said, staring down the street from the railroad station. "I thought every town in the West would be like—"

"Dodge City?" Slocum finished for her. "Denver's got well nigh a hundred thousand people in it. There's an opera house with a company as good as anything in New York. Or so I'm told," he added hastily. Slocum wasn't a fan of opera and had never been to the Denver opera house. And he certainly had no idea of what the music was like back in New York City.

"Well, yes. There are so many people, and they all look prosperous." Ruth blinked when a streetcar rattled past the station.

Slocum did some quick figuring and wondered what would be the best course for them. Buying horses and gear in Denver might prove to be better than taking the train to Cheyenne, and then buying mounts. The farther north, the higher the price. But he had to balance the expense with the ease of travel for Ruth. She would hold up better sitting in a rattling train than she would on the trail.

"We can see when the next train north is," Slocum said. "That will be easier and quicker than riding straight for Devils Tower."

"Do not worry about me, John. I am able to ride a horse. I may appear to be a hothouse flower, but I've accompanied Father many times on his trips. Some were under quite . . . severe conditions."

Slocum shrugged. He turned over the paths open to him and decided the added speed of getting north would be a boon, not a detriment. Ruth Waddell had the money for high-priced horses in Cheyenne, and he wanted to keep ahead of Bronston and Dickensen.

At the thought of the Union soldiers, he looked over his shoulder and back down the tracks in the direction of Kansas. Slocum laughed off his uneasiness. The next train from Dodge City wasn't due for two days. Even if Bronston had taken off hell-bent for leather, he couldn't have matched the railroad's time getting to Denver.

"We can take the train north," Slocum said decisively. "I'll see about some provisions here so we won't pay through the nose once we get on the frontier."

"On the frontier," Ruth said, rolling the phrase over and over as if it were hot on her tongue. "Very well. Will you see to finding those who have spoken with Father here?"

"No need," Slocum said. "Iron Foot was pretty sure Devils Tower was your father's destination. I'm sure there are people here in Denver who remember him, but unless something bad happened, he'll have gone on north."

"Perhaps so, but I will make inquiries. I remember a few names Father mentioned before starting for the frontier." Ruth looked around as if unsure how to proceed.

"You go on and take a carriage," Slocum said. "I'll find a store to get supplies and see them loaded on the train." He checked the schedule posted over the ticket agent's booth. "The Cheyenne Express leaves at sundown."

"I shall be back before then. How will I find you if I return sooner?" A touch of apprehension entered her words now. Ruth didn't want to be alone, even in a city as civilized as Denver.

"It won't take me an hour to find what we need. I'll be here on the platform waiting for you."

"Very well." Ruth paused and looked at him. He tried to read what was in her brown eyes and couldn't. "Thank you for understanding." She stood on tiptoe and gave him a quick kiss.

Slocum looked around to be sure no one had seen. It would ruin a lady's reputation being seen kissing like this in public. No one had noticed.

Ruth Waddell hurried off to look up her father's business acquaintances. Slocum heaved a sigh, touched the money he had in his shirt pocket, and cursed himself for not asking Ruth for money to buy supplies. Still, he reckoned she was good for it, and she had already helped him out of a tight spot back in Dodge City. He set out to find a general store that wouldn't rob him of his eyeteeth.

• • •

"John! John!" Ruth Waddell's insistent calls brought him out of his sleep. He had been dreaming of green pastures and wide-open vistas. Slocum pushed himself up to a sitting position next to the pile of supplies he'd bought.

"Over here," he said, pushing his Stetson back onto his head. He got to his feet, stretched, and looked at the clock. The train was going to leave at seven-thirty. It was almost six o'clock.

"I'm so glad I found you," Ruth said breathlessly. She was flushed and looked more excited than Slocum could remember seeing her—except once.

"What's got you so riled?"

"John, he's still in Denver. He didn't go north!"

"Slow down," Slocum said, wondering what was going on. From all he had heard of Phillip Waddell, the man was possessed of a one-track mind. If he wanted pictures of Devils Tower, he'd get them come hell or high water. He wasn't likely to stick around Denver for any length of time.

Ruth took a deep breath. Slocum appreciated the way her bosom rose and fell, but forced himself to concentrate on her words anyway.

"Mr. Michaels said he saw Father just this morning. He said—"

"Who's this Michaels fellow?" Slocum interrupted.

"I went to a photographer who my father has corresponded with and met Mr. Michaels there."

"But Michaels isn't the one your father wrote to? He's someone else?" Slocum didn't like the sound of this.

"That's right. Anyway, please listen, John. Mr. Michaels says that Father is staying at the Fairmont Square Hotel and that we can meet him there in a few minutes." Ruth glanced at the clock on the station house wall.

"We're meeting Michaels or your father? Or both?"

"Mr. Michaels said Father would be there."

Slocum scratched his head and looked around. They had almost ninety minutes before the train for Cheyenne left. There was time to check out the story and see if Phillip Waddell was registered at the hotel, and make sure this was not some sort of wild-goose chase.

"Where is this hotel? Buildings pop up like toadstools in Denver. I don't remember hearing of it."

"That's the good thing," Ruth rushed on. "It's only a few minutes away from here—from the railroad station—here." She was beside herself with eagerness to find her father.

"Wait a minute," Slocum said. He went to the ticket booth and spoke with the agent. He returned and said, "The hotel's not more than a half mile away. I don't reckon it would hurt to check and see if your pa's there."

Something bothered Slocum, but he couldn't put his finger on it.

"Don't worry so, John," said Ruth. "I'll give you your money for helping me. Here, you can have it now." She fumbled in her purse and handed him the money.

"There's no need for this now," Slocum started. He saw Ruth wasn't listening. She wanted to see her father again. Slocum stuffed the bills into his shirt pocket and said, "There's a carriage. Let's get there quickly so we can still catch the train if this Michaels was wrong."

"How could he be wrong?" Ruth demanded. "He described Father accurately. He *must* have seen him recently."

Slocum rode along silently. The Fairmont Square Hotel was a three-story structure that must have been built within the past year. Slocum's nose wrinkled as he imagined he smelled still-drying mortar between the red bricks. He held the hotel's beveled glass door open for Ruth. He followed her, heading for the clerk standing behind a long, oak desk. Slocum paused when he heard someone call out Ruth's name. He turned and saw a weasellike man rush from the lobby to intercept her.

"Mr. Michaels, I hadn't expected to see you here," Ruth said.

"Something's come up. Something you need to tend to right away," Michaels said. His eyes darted in Slocum's direction and back.

"This is Mr. Slocum. He is aiding me in finding Father."

"Slocum, eh?" Michaels shook his head. "Don't matter if he comes along, I guess. He wants to meet you out back."

"Out back?" Ruth asked. "How strange."

"He's been hurt. Not bad, not bad," Michaels hastened to say, "but he needs to see you something fierce."

Ruth rushed out with Michaels in the lead. Slocum followed at a distance, flipping the leather thong off the hammer of his Colt Navy. He didn't like this at all.

"There he is, Miss Waddell. Go to him."

In the alley lay a man covered with a blanket. The man stirred and moaned softly. Ruth rushed to his side and bent down. Slocum took a step forward, then turned for Michaels. He sensed a trap—but was still taken in.

A heavy blow to the top of his head sent John Slocum pitching forward into black oblivion.

7

Slocum tried to yell, but he couldn't. He tried to sit up, but he could only thrash weakly on the ground. When he fought to bring his hands around in front of him to help sit up, he felt an intense pressure in his shoulders that told him he was bound securely.

Slowly, the awareness of his surroundings came back. He was gagged, and someone had savagely tied his wrists with wire. Blinking sweat from his eyes, he felt wooden planking against his face. Groaning, he forced himself over onto his back, and for a horrifying instant, he thought he was blind.

Then he realized he was in a dark room. Slocum strained to get whatever information he could about his prison without moving further. Details began to fit together, and he realized that he was tied up and dumped in a closed boxcar. With this knowledge, he felt a little more secure. Slocum thrashed around until he came to a wall. Using it, he levered himself into a sitting position.

Like his wrists, his ankles were bound securely with wire, but his boots protected him from the flesh-cutting viciousness. Still, he knew the wire cutting into his boots would prevent him from going far.

Slocum froze when he heard scraping noises from a few feet away. He squinted and tried to make out what was moving. Rats would rip out his throat and strip his carcass. He had seen rats bigger than dogs running loose around rail yards. Again came the sound, and this time he heard a sob with it. For the first time, the haze completely cleared from Slocum's throbbing head and he remembered how he had ended up in this predicament.

He remembered Ruth Waddell had been with him.

The sobs turned to mumbled words, and he knew Ruth was similarly tied and gagged.

He rolled in her direction and fetched up hard against her. She recoiled and let out a startled "Umm!" before settling down and seeing what had happened. Slocum thrust out his chin and rubbed it against her arm, trying to get his message through. Eyes adjusting to the dim light, he saw her nod her head in understanding. Slocum worked his way down her arm until his gag pressed hard against her fingers.

Cold lumps stroked his face. He realized they had both been bound long enough for the circulation to stop in both their hands and feet. They had to escape quickly or they would never be able to use their fingers for unfastening their bonds.

"There!" he gasped out as she pulled the gag free of his mouth. "I can breathe better. Thanks."

He was greeted with passionate sobs. Slocum knew what Ruth wanted. They reversed positions, and he freed her from her gag.

"I was choking to death, John. What happened?"

"I was going to ask you that. We went into the alley, you bent over your father, and I saw your face. I turned toward Michaels, and the lights went out."

"It wasn't Father," she said glumly. "Some man I'd never

seen before reached up and grabbed me. Mr. Michaels lied to me!"

Slocum had already figured out who was responsible for the ambush. Bronston had telegraphed ahead to Michaels to order the man to bushwhack them, and Slocum had walked into the trap with his eyes wide open. It wasn't Ruth's place to look for such snares; it was his, and he had failed. He cursed Samuel Morse for inventing the damned thing.

"We've got to get out of here or we're dead," Slocum told her. "This is all Bronston's doing. He wants to keep us from reaching your father."

"But why?"

"I don't know, but it has to be important to Bronston to go to such trouble."

"Where are we?"

"I hope we're still in Denver," Slocum said. He told her what he had figured out as he fought against the wire binding his wrists. Slocum felt blood begin to trickle down into his palms. He was injuring himself trying to get free.

"This Major Bronston," asked Ruth, "what will he do with us?"

"He might want to kill us himself," Slocum said, but he wondered. Bronston didn't seem the kind to let obstacles get in his way. If his underlings could remove them, fine. Slocum had seen the way he ordered Dickensen around. The sergeant enjoyed getting blood on his hands. Unless he missed his guess, Slocum thought that Bronston considered killing nothing more than an inconvenience. Bronston would kill and never think twice, but he didn't revel in it like his henchman did.

Slocum decided he and Ruth were safe—for a spell.

"He might just want us out of the way," Slocum said, thinking aloud. "Or maybe Michaels chickened out."

"You mean he was supposed to kill us and didn't?" Ruth

was astounded at the notion of dying in this manner.

"Maybe, but Michaels didn't look to be all that squeamish about killing, and he had the chance when we were both knocked out."

"John, I'm sorry," Ruth said, beginning to cry. "I should never have sought out Father's friends."

"Michaels was waiting for you," Slocum said. "If he hadn't found you at the photographer's studio, he would have bumped into you some other way."

"What are we going to do?"

"First we get free of the wire on our wrists," Slocum said, but he didn't know how.

For almost an hour he worked. He tried to loosen Ruth's bonds but failed, then he let her try to work his free—and she failed. He often collapsed, exhausted from the effort. During these times he listened intently, hoping a conductor would come by to check the boxcar. A railroad worker should come by, unless the car was deserted on a siding. But no one came near. When he saw the faint fingers of dawn poking through the planks in the car's roof he knew they were in trouble.

The next train from Dodge City would be arriving in a few hours, and he didn't doubt that Bronston and his men would be aboard.

"John, do you see that? Over in the corner? Is it what I think it is?"

Slocum worked around to see what Ruth had found. His heart almost exploded with relief. A crimping tool lay there. He rolled over to the tool and grabbed for it, only to be slammed hard against the wall. It took him a second to realize he had lost his balance because the boxcar was starting to move.

"John, where are we going?" cried Ruth.

"I don't know," he said, "but it looks as if Bronston

wanted us shanghaied. We've got to get off this train as fast as possible." He doubled his effort to get the crimping tool. The cool metal slid through his blood-slickened, numbed fingers several times before he got a good grip on it.

"What can I do?" cried Ruth, almost in tears.

"Sit as still as you can," Slocum told her. He wiggled around and found the wires around her slender wrists. She yelped when he missed and got skin. He finally found the strand holding everything together and snipped through it.

"Thank heavens!" Ruth exclaimed, falling to one side. "My hands are so cold, so paralyzed."

"Wiggle them—and get me free!" Slocum demanded. He squirmed as she took her time getting his bonds cut. He rubbed his lacerated wrists and winced at the pain arrowing into his arms. Slocum took the crimping tool, which was used by railway workers to fasten locks on the boxcar doors, and cut the wire around his ankles. He finished off Ruth's bonds with another quick snip and got to his feet shakily.

"We're rolling along at a goodly clip," he told her, pressing his eye against a crack in the boxcar's door. "I can't be sure, but I think we're heading south."

"South? To Mexico?"

"New Mexico Territory. Probably Lamy, to the AT and SF railhead there. We're not too far out of Denver, though. We've got to get out of the freight car and get back."

Slocum tried to force open the door but it was securely fastened outside. Every rumble and clank of the steel wheels, and every whine of the whistle took him farther away from Denver. He was all too aware of the emptiness at his left hip where his Colt Navy had once rested. His shirt pocket was devoid of money and, worst of all, Michaels, or the men working with him, had stolen his watch.

The gun and money Slocum might have forgiven, but never would he rest until he got that watch back. It had belonged to his brother Robert, who was killed during that fool Pickett's charge off Little Roundtop. Other than memories, it was all Slocum had of his brother.

"John, look!" exclaimed Ruth. She knelt where they had been tied. Her fingers picked at a loose plank in the floor. "I can't get it out—help me!"

Slocum dropped beside the brunette and added his strength to hers. The wooden plank yielded with a loud groaning sound, then popped free. Slocum tumbled back with Ruth beside him. She had a broad grin on her face. In spite of the grime and a few cuts, Slocum had never seen a more beautiful woman. He kissed her quickly.

"John," she said, "do you want to. . . ."

"Not here, not now. We have to get off the train." He helped her to her feet. The racing tracks under the boxcar's wheels showed through the boards. Getting off would be dangerous. He lowered himself through the hole and felt hot cinders kicked up off the roadbed. With his feet kicking, he found the steel rods under the car that sometimes afforded free passage for the daring. Riding the rails was dangerous but it could be done if he kept his nerve.

"Be careful," Ruth said needlessly. Slocum wasn't going to get himself killed—not yet. He had a score to settle.

"I'll try to get the door open from the outside. Be ready to jump. It feels as if the train is slowing."

Slocum swung down, and hooked his long legs over a rod. He lowered himself slowly and then found a place to grip. Inching across the bottom of the car with the flying ties and cinders just inches under his back, he got to the side of the boxcar. Here he found iron handgrips and pulled himself up.

He let out a sigh of relief. The freight car's door wasn't locked, it was only closed with a simple hasp. Slocum worked his way across the side of the car and flipped the hasp away from its staple. Ruth opened the door immediately.

"Let's go," he called, grabbing her hand.

"Wait, John, I want to—"

He didn't give her time to worry about the jump. The train was rounding a long curve. In flat country like this, the train would pick up speed again once it straightened out, and this would make leaving even more dangerous. Slocum wanted to take full advantage of the curve. They hit the ground hand in hand, and rolled down a small incline.

"I never did anything like that before," Ruth said, shaking her head.

"Are you all right?" Slocum got up and dusted himself off. He had picked a good spot not only to jump off the train, but also to get on to the next one northbound. The sharp curve forced any train to slow.

"Fine. How do we get back to Denver?" Ruth tried to fix her hair but her chestnut mane was in wild disarray. Slocum smiled as he saw her trying to tuck the vagrant strands back. She looked lovely.

"Reverse the jump. We get on when one comes from the south. I don't remember the schedule too well, but it shouldn't be long. It's a busy route between Denver and Colorado Springs. The express ought to get past the Springs in an hour. Give the returning train another hour."

"Two hours to sit out here?" she asked in disgust. The land was flat, hot, and dry, with only the Rockies rising to the west to break the monotony.

"If we put our minds to it, we ought to find a way to pass the time," Slocum said. And they did.

Ruth Waddell lounged back after their lovemaking and stared into the azure sky. "I understand what Father sees in this country. It's gorgeous. There's nothing like it back East."

Slocum shrugged. He'd never been back East, at least not to New York, or Boston, or any place north of the Mason-Dixon Line. He started to tell her about the last time he'd ridden through Colorado on his way to Leadville and its fabulous gold mines when he sat bolt upright. Cocking his head to one side he strained to hear the distant sound more clearly.

"Get dressed," he ordered. "There's a train coming."

"But it hasn't been two hours," Ruth protested.

"There must be a feeder line I don't know about," Slocum said, pulling on his jeans. His hand touched the empty spot at his hip and he remembered he'd lost his Colt. For the moment.

He scrambled up the slope and put his ear to the steel rails. The hum told him the train wasn't far away. Standing, he saw a column of black rising from the engine's smokestack.

"Get ready. We will only have one chance to board."

The train neared. Ruth came up the slope and stood beside Slocum. She reached out and put her hand on his arm.

"John, whatever happens, I want to thank you."

"All that's going to happen right now is us getting a ride back to Denver." Slocum braced himself for the leap onto the train. The engine had to slow for the curve but it still chugged along at a respectable speed.

"There, go for the freight car's open door," he told her. Slocum gauged the distance, then turned and ran a few steps parallel to the tracks. The car flashed past and he jumped, catching the edge of the door and swinging around into the car.

Ruth ran as fast as she could but couldn't quite reach the edge of the open door. Slocum threw himself flat on the boxcar's floor and reached out, grabbing the woman's wrist. He gave a powerful tug that brought her tumbling into the car.

"We made it," she gasped out. "We did it!"

"Reckon you two done something, all right," came the cold words. "And I don't much like it."

Ruth and Slocum spun around to see a six-shooter leveled at them. The hammer came back with a noise louder than the clattering steel wheels under them or the shrill whistle in front.

8

"I wouldn't want to drill you, but I will," the man said. He moved slightly to keep Slocum silhouetted in the freight car door before turning to study Ruth. "My, my, ain't you a frisky filly?"

"Let her be," Slocum said.

"Now why would I do a think like that?" the man asked. Slocum squinted and let his eyes adjust to the dimness inside the car. He caught glints of sunlight off bright brass buttons. For a terrible moment, he thought he had run afoul of Major Bronston again. As his vision adapted, he saw that they had been caught by the train's conductor.

"You jumped the train. You ought to pay."

"We'll pay," Slocum said, trying to distract the conductor's attention from Ruth. "We just couldn't make it to the nearest station to buy a ticket all properlike."

To Slocum's surprise, the conductor laughed loudly and let the hammer on his six-gun down gently. He stuck the pistol back into his right jacket pocket.

"I do declare, Slocum, you are about the best person on this whole earth to make fun of. You take everything too damned serious for your own good."

The conductor came over and clapped Slocum on the

shoulder. Only then did Slocum get a good look at him.

"Pete Newcomb! I thought that posse down in Ouray stretched your neck good and proper."

"They don't call me Sneaky Pete for nothing, Slocum. I must say the quality of your travelin' companions has improved a sight since we rode together a year or two back." The conductor touched the brim of his cap and grinned at Ruth.

"You know one another?" Ruth was still paralyzed by the sight of Newcomb's six-shooter. "You acted as if we were common hoodlums and—"

"Don't mind her, Pete. What are you doing in that getup?" Slocum asked, giving his friend the once-over. "You haven't gone honest—have you?"

"Of course I have, Slocum. It gets lonely out there, the law all the time doggin' your heels. You know that." Newcomb glanced at Ruth, and wondered if *she* knew Slocum's checkered background. Ruth made no indication of surprise at what Newcomb hinted about Slocum.

"What's the truth of it, Pete? You were always crookeder than a dog's hind leg."

"Look who's talkin'," Newcomb said without rancor. He squatted down, his back to the wooden side of the freight car. "This is a real soft job, Slocum."

"Commandeering freight? Overcharging passengers?" Slocum knew his old friend wasn't going straight.

"That goes without saying," Newcomb allowed. "The real money comes in carrying extra cargo nobody else knows about. You'd be surprised how often a gent has to get out of Denver or the Springs and doesn't want anyone knowing."

"Is that what you're doing back here?" asked Ruth. "You were checking on contraband shipments?"

Newcomb laughed uproariously at Ruth's comment.

"Might be, little lady. Don't say much about my business. I'm like Slocum in that way. But you'd better answer my questions. What are you doing jumping freight trains out in the middle of nowhere?"

"We were shanghaied," Slocum said. He quickly explained and then asked, "Do you know anyone named Michaels in Denver?"

"Does he look like a blue-tailed skink out sunnin' hisself on a jagged rock?"

"He has a certain resemblance to a lizard," Slocum said.

Newcomb snorted in disgust. "I'd give him what for myself, if I could. He's nothing but a backshootin', scum-sucking son of a bitch, 'scuse my French, ma'am. Yeah, I know him. Got into a poker game with him and a couple of his cohorts a month back." Newcomb stretched his left arm in obvious pain. "About all I got out of the game was an empty pocket and a bullet I'm still carryin' in my shoulder."

"Oh, dear," Ruth said.

"Don't fret none over it, ma'am," Newcomb said. "That shoulder always seizes up when the weather changes. Better than any barometer, and it'll come in right handy during the winter months. Never did abide by blizzards."

"Where can I find him?" Slocum tried to keep the steel edge out of his voice. From the way Newcomb's eyes narrowed, he knew he hadn't done too good a job. Pete could read him like a book. It was a good thing they'd always gotten along or Slocum would have had to kill him for that.

"You might try the Baron's Retreat, just off Larrimer Square. Crooked gaming house. Don't know for certain but I'd wager a pile that Michaels owns part of the action." Newcomb leaned out the door and ducked back. "We're almost into the yard. You'd better get off 'fore then."

"Railroad detectives?" asked Slocum.

"Thicker'n fleas on a dirty dog," Newcomb answered.

"That's why I don't have any freight on this run. It's amazing what a few greenbacks put into the right hand will get you."

"Thanks, Newcomb," said Slocum. "I'd be more'n happy to push a few dollars your way, but Michaels robbed us blind."

"Consider it my due when you pay him back." Newcomb looked out the door again, then said, "You'd better take this. Michaels is a no-account backshooter." Newcomb reached into his pocket and handed over his six-shooter.

"But it's your pistol, Mr. Newcomb!" protested Ruth. "We could never take it."

"You got yourself a good one in her, Slocum." Quicker than a flash, Newcomb had two more six-guns yanked from hiding places in his uniform. "This here's a dangerous run. Never let it be said Old Sneaky Pete was stupid enough to make it without at least three six-guns."

Slocum took Ruth's arm and guided her to the door. As the train rounded a bend to make its final entry into the rail yard, he jumped, pulling Ruth behind him. They hit and rolled, coming to a sitting position in the cinders. Ruth choked, but Slocum couldn't waste time now waiting for her to ease up.

"The railroad detectives might be looking for us," he said. "If Bronston knew enough about Denver to hire Michaels, he might have hired Pinkertons to keep an eye out for us trying to sneak back."

"I doubt that," Ruth said, brushing herself off. "Bronston has no cause to think we are any place other than Lamy."

"Don't know why he didn't have Michaels just kill us. Are you sure you don't know Bronston or Dickensen?"

"No, and I don't know why they would do this to us." Ruth swallowed hard. "And I most assuredly do not know why they want to speak with Father."

Slocum didn't tell the brunette Bronston wasn't the talking kind. Whatever business he had with Phillip Waddell, it was of the killing variety. Looking around, he saw a way out of the yard. They hiked over some tracks and finally reached a point a half mile outside Denver's city limits.

"Where I'm going will be rough. Why don't you stay—" Slocum never got to finish. Ruth stamped her foot and put her hands on her hips.

"I will not," she said firmly. "I want to see what happens to that terrible Mr. Michaels. He *lied* to me."

Slocum considered what might happen. Leaving Ruth behind was almost as bad as having her with him, but at least he could watch after her. He fingered the six-shooter Newcomb had given him. It was short-barreled and a small caliber, but it would do if he got close enough to Michaels. If nothing else, the flare from the powder would set fire to Michaels's clothing.

"Walk fast. I've got this feeling time is working against us." Slocum hiked in silence, trying to figure out if Bronston and Dickensen could have reached Denver yet. Possibly so. He couldn't be sure. He and Ruth had been on their detour for almost a full day. By the time they got into Denver, the sun was dipping behind the Front Range and the city was getting cooler.

It would heat up when they got to the Baron's Retreat.

"There, there it is," Ruth said, pointing after they had wandered around Larrimer Square for almost twenty minutes. She indicated a crudely lettered wooden sign depicting an English nobleman playing cards. Slocum held her back. She would blunder straight into the den of thieves without a second thought.

"We watch for a few minutes. I need to know who goes in, and I need to see how they come out."

"Oh, you want to know of any back doors or secret

ways." This seemed to calm Ruth. She stood quietly as Slocum watched the slow march of men go in and out of the gambling house. The riffraff went in the front and came out the back, usually beaten and unconscious. The higher class customers either left the way they entered, or stayed.

Slocum saw lights wink on and off in second-story windows. The cribs were up there for the well-heeled customers.

After twenty minutes, Slocum said, "I'm going inside. I've seen enough to be able to get out in a hurry—if it comes to that."

"Very well." Ruth Waddell started after him. Slocum stopped and looked at her as if she had lost her mind.

"You can't go in there," he said. "There's only one type of woman who is seen in a gambling house."

"Cyprians," Ruth said softly, her brown eyes glowing. "I know. Don't you think I could pass as a soiled dove?" She did a pirouette and showed a bit of ankle. "Don't I look pretty enough?"

Slocum saw that nothing would dissuade her. "Stay close and don't be shocked at anything you see. All we're after is Michaels and some information." Slocum silently added his Colt Navy, the stolen money, and his brother's watch to the list. He didn't think it wise to burden Ruth with too many details.

They entered, and the doorman gave Ruth a knowing leer. To Slocum's surprise, she reached out to stroke the doorman's cheek and made as if she was going to kiss him. Slocum grabbed her wrist and pulled her along, while laughing heartily.

"Shocked, John?" she whispered. "Am I acting like a lady of ill repute?"

"They call them whores," he said harshly. Slocum didn't want a fight starting over her actions. Still, they had gotten inside without arousing any suspicion. If anything, Ruth's action had put any doubts the bouncer had to rest. No proper lady would do what Ruth had done.

He stopped just inside the door to the smoke-filled room. It was hard to see far because of the heavy cigar smoke, but Slocum heard a shrill voice he recognized immediately. Still holding Ruth by the wrist, he pulled her across the room. Sitting at a table and dealing Spanish monte was the man he sought.

Ruth started to go to Michaels, but Slocum held her back. He whispered in her ear. She recoiled in horror, then slowly smiled. He hadn't known how she would react to his suggestion. Slocum was pleased that Ruth was going to go along with it without showing any signs of moral indignation at such lewd behavior.

If anything, she seemed to be enjoying herself.

Ruth Waddell strutted to Michaels and laid a hand on his shoulder. The man jerked around, and his hand went for a pistol. Slocum stiffened when he saw the six-shooter, the ebony handle of his Colt Navy didn't belong stuck in Michaels's waistband.

She bent over and whispered quickly in Michaels's ear, not letting him get a good look at her face. The weasellike man sneered and quickly raked in his money from the table, over the protests of the other players.

"Where, baby?" Slocum heard Michaels ask Ruth. Michaels's attention was divided between his money, the players, and Ruth.

"Out back. You won't regret it." She heaved a deep sigh and said, "You don't know how much I need you right now." Ruth turned and quickly left.

"They all do, they all do," Michaels called after her. Slocum followed, but he had to act the instant he reached the alleyway behind the club. Michaels had already spun

Ruth around and had his hand under her skirt, more intent on what he found there than who she was.

Slocum pulled out the small pistol Newcomb had given him and hauled off. The short barrel smashed into the side of Michaels's head, driving the man to his knees. In spite of the unexpected attack, Michaels groped for Slocum's six-shooter. To their surprise, Ruth had wrenched it free. She held it in both hands with its muzzle thrust hard against the side of Michaels's face.

"Give me a reason not to shoot," she said, her voice trembling.

"I'll give you one," Slocum said. "He's mine." He snared his Colt from her and swung it around. Both barrels were trained on Michaels.

"What—You can't rob me. *Me*! I—oh dear God, no!" Michaels saw the tombstones in Slocum's eyes, and they had his name chiseled on them.

"I didn't mean to do it, honest," the man protested, finally recognizing Slocum and Ruth. "He made me do it. I saw you two were good people." Michaels stared at Ruth in disbelief. He had responded to her indecent proposal and hadn't recognized her until now.

"I've got my Colt back," Slocum said. "Now give us the money." He used Newcomb's pistol to poke around Michaels's jacket until he found his stash. The man almost ripped the pocket off fumbling to get it out.

"How much was it? A hundred? Two? Lemme count it out." Hands shaking, Michaels counted off half the roll. Slocum swung the barrel of Newcomb's pistol and cracked a bone in Michaels's wrist. The man dropped all the money to the alley floor.

"Take it all, Ruth," Slocum ordered. "We deserve it for our trouble."

"Look, don't kill me, mister. Bronston made me do it.

He told me to kill you. I didn't do that. I just throwed you onto the train and—"

"Quit lying," Slocum said. "And give me back my watch."

Fear flooded Michaels. He stammered out, "I ain't got it. Bronston took it as a souvenir; as proof I done you in. The man's crazy, I tell you. He don't take scalps. He always takes something else, something to prove it was a man he killed. He's crazy!"

"He has my watch?" Slocum's finger tensed on the Colt's hair trigger. There was no need to keep this worthless sidewinder alive one second longer.

"I can show you where he is. I can take you to him. Don't kill me!"

"John, wait," said Ruth. She had a change of heart concerning Michaels, and Slocum saw it instantly. "I have a better idea."

Slocum had to agree.

"Don't kill me, please," pleaded Michaels. "You don't know what a devil Bronston is—and that sergeant of his! Dickensen is worse!"

"This ought to keep him quiet," Ruth said. She shoved an oily rag into his mouth and picked up a loop of wire. The brunette paused a moment, and let the wire brush over Michaels's throat. She shook her head; wanton killing wasn't in her. She lifted the loop until it held the gag firmly in place.

Slocum secured Michaels's hands behind him with more wire he'd found in the rail yard. Only then did he step back and look appraisingly at their captive.

"You want to do it?" He handed Newcomb's pistol to Ruth.

Fear flared in Michaels's face. Slocum had no sympathy for the man. There was no telling how many people the bushwhacking gambler had killed. For whatever reason, he hadn't killed them, and that was proving to be a big mistake on his part.

"You do it," Ruth said. "I want to watch."

Slocum yanked hard and stripped off Michaels's shirt. Then he tore off the top part of the man's filthy union suit sending buttons sailing in all directions. He jerked off Michaels's boots and trousers, then finished getting the long underwear off him. Michaels lay naked and trembling in the cinder of the rail yard.

"There is the boxcar Mr. Newcomb prepared," Ruth said, pointing to an open freight car. "Let's get him aboard."

Slocum hoisted Michaels to his feet and shoved him into the freight car. He fell heavily to the floor, groaned, and rolled over with anger burning in his eyes. Slocum couldn't understand what their captive was saying, but he could guess.

He tossed Newcomb's gun into the car so that it lay alongside Michaels.

"Train's pulling out," Slocum said. "The owner of that six-shooter will be along to claim it in a few minutes."

Straining, he shoved the heavy boxcar door shut and dropped the hasp over the staple. A turn of wire would keep it from being opened.

"What will your friend do to him?" Ruth asked.

"Can't rightly say. It depends on how riled Newcomb was over their poker game." Slocum stood back and watched the train pull out of the yard. Atop one car he saw the conductor, Pete Newcomb, waving to them, in recognition of their gift to him. Then the train turned a bend and built up speed.

Slocum had recovered his Colt Navy. Now he had to track down Bronston and get his watch back, and find Phillip Waddell somewhere along the way. And this time, blood would flow.

9

"Don't we have an awful lot of gear?" Ruth Waddell asked. "I should think you would want to travel light."

Slocum shook his head. He had four horses; two for riding and two for resting. Then he'd gone and bought a sturdy pack mule to carry their supplies. By switching mounts when their horses got tired, he reckoned they could make better time to Cheyenne than they could by waiting days for the next train.

There was something else he was loath to mention to Ruth. If Bronston had alerted anyone along the way to look for them, they'd be sitting ducks on a train. By taking off across country, Slocum not only felt better, but would be able to see trouble coming.

"We can make better time. I'm guessing Bronston and Dickensen took last night's train." A train had left for Cheyenne just minutes before they had arrived back in Denver from their daylong detour. Slocum had made inquiries, and the train was on a milk run. It'd stop at every whistle-stop between Denver and Cheyenne.

"I don't see how that is possible. And do we really need four horses?" She eyed the large animals with some distaste. For all her claiming that she knew how to ride, Slocum guessed the opposite was true. She may have ridden a gentled mare, but never a horse born and bred for the frontier.

"We do," he said. "I'm even thinking of spending another fifty dollars and getting a spare mule." Slocum still had money left. He had taken more than seven hundred dollars from Michaels before stripping him and leaving him to Pete Newcomb's tender mercy. This was about the only time Slocum could remember coming out ahead after making such a bad error in judgment.

"I will concede that you know more than I," Ruth said primly, "but it would be more comfortable riding the train to Cheyenne, even if we do have to wait another day or two."

"Your father might not have the luxury of a day or two," Slocum told her. "Bronston might be closer to him than we are. You've seen how ruthless the major is. What's his business with your pa?"

"I . . . you are right, John. I'm sorry for doubting you. It's just that this is a most daunting trip for me." Ruth came over and put her arms around Slocum, hugging him. He felt wet spots on his shirt where she cried.

He held her uneasily for a moment, then pushed her back. "We'll find your father before Bronston. But I'm asking something more in the way of payment."

Ruth Waddell stiffened. "What is that?"

"I want your pa to take a picture of us together, you and me. I don't remember ever wanting my photograph taken before, but this seems like a good time."

"Oh, John, you always surprise me so!" She gave him another hug, then stepped back. "Now show me how to saddle this brute. There is so much I need to learn."

"Not one inch farther!" Ruth Waddell protested. "I have ridden until I am so sore I cannot sit another second." She lifted herself enough in the stirrups to rub her bottom. Under other circumstances, Slocum might have enjoyed watching this. He kept scanning the horizon, and worried about time slipping away.

They had been on the trail two days and had made good time, considering that Ruth's inexperience slowed their pace considerably. He estimated they had gone better than sixty miles, switching horses frequently to keep any one animal from getting too tuckered out. The mule plodded along with their supplies, its long ears flopping back and forth to keep the summertime flies away. Other than this, the mule gave no sign of strain at the pace.

"We can't take the time to rest," he said. "Bronston is ahead of us. He might already be in Cheyenne. The northbound train might stop at every town along the way, but it's able to keep a pace we can't hope to match."

"We're not following the railroad tracks," Ruth protested. "We're cutting miles and miles off by going straight across country. You said so yourself. Or have you forgotten?"

"I haven't forgotten anything," Slocum said, reaching over to touch his ebony-handled Colt Navy, just to reassure himself it was still there. The empty vest pocket where he usually carried his brother's watch taunted him with every mile, though.

Major Bronston had the watch, and Slocum was going to get it back come hell or high water.

"There's no need to kill ourselves. We would be of no use to Father if we arrived so tired we could hardly stand." Ruth swung her leg over the saddle horn and slid to the ground. She moaned softly and rubbed her butt again. "I am taking a break. You may do so, or not, as you see fit."

"Make camp for the night," Slocum said, even though it was only mid afternoon. "I'll do some scouting. I think we can reach Cheyenne in a day, if we can find the right pass through the Laramie Mountains. Then it'll be about two hundred fifty miles to Devils Tower." Slocum had no idea how long that would take due to the number of rivers to ford. If spring runoff was high, they might have problems, but from what he'd seen it had been a dry year and not much snow dotted the tops of the tallest mountains.

"Very well," Ruth said. She went to the mule and began unpacking it. The animal balked, and she stepped back warily. The brunette had almost been kicked by the mule the day before and only approached it hesitantly.

Slocum shook his head. No matter how she tried, Ruth Waddell would never be at home away from the big city and all its comforts. He rode a mile or two, then cut to the west, hunting for a rise to use his spyglass. The mountain range rising to the north would hold them back many days unless he found the right pass.

Pulling out the small spyglass he'd bought to replace the one left in Dodge City, he put it to his eye and scanned the horizon. Through the clutter of pines and low growth, he made out several possible trails, but Slocum couldn't be sure. He smiled when he saw a well-traveled road meandering upward through a pass not ten miles distant. They could have made the pass if Ruth hadn't been as balky as the mule.

Slocum almost put the spyglass down when he noticed a tiny puff of dust rising along the trail. Frowning, he tried to hold the spyglass steady to see what caused the small disturbance. His gelding danced to and fro, trying to crow hop. Unable to gentle the horse so he could use the spyglass Slocum dismounted and tethered the horse on a low chokeberry bush.

He found the fork of a juniper and rested the spyglass in it. For several minutes he saw no sign of other travelers along the path. He started to fold the spyglass and put it into his saddlebags when he noticed a movement. Settling down and watching intently, he saw a sight that made him catch his breath and involuntarily hold it.

Expelling the air when his lungs threatened to burst, Slocum muttered, "Ute!"

Ten minutes later he was still watching as the band of Indians trickled past in knots of two and three braves. He had seen hunting parties and war parties before, and this wasn't a hunting party. Whatever had riled the Utes had caused them to send out a war party of better than thirty warriors.

The last of the braves vanished from his sight, and Slocum sat down with the spyglass across his knees. He took a deep breath, got to his feet, and mounted. Seeing the war party put him on guard. He had a goodly bit of scouting to do to make certain they weren't surprised in their camp by another band of Utes. It took the better part of the afternoon but Slocum convinced himself they were safe.

He rode into camp to find Ruth working at starting a fire. Dismounting, he went over and took the lucifers from her.

"No fire tonight. We have a cold camp."

"John, really! There is no reason to torture me as you are doing. I am doing my level best to keep up. I know I cannot match your skill but—"

"Utes," he said. "A war party of better than thirty braves is less than a half day ahead of us. They'll be through the pass by the time we get there tomorrow, but tonight we sit tight and let them go their way."

"We would have run into them, wouldn't we? If I hadn't insisted we stop, our scalps would be hanging on their belts!" Ruth was aghast at this.

"Not exactly," Slocum told her. "My scalp would be theirs." He said nothing more, letting the impact of his words sink in. He would be dead. Ruth would be a captive.

He opened two cans of beans and handed one to the woman. She took it and poked at the contents listlessly, then finally put it aside. Ruth looked squarely at him and asked, "Is it worth the effort, John?"

"You tell me," he answered between mouthfuls of beans. "You're the one who has to tell your father about your mother's death. Can it wait?"

"No, not really," Ruth said, looking more morose by the minute. "He deserves to know, and you can see how hard he is to track down. I'm sorry I started on this insane chase, but I'm glad I'm here. Does that make any sense?"

"In a way," Slocum said. "I started looking for your father for money. Now I'm going to find him—and Bronston."

"You want to kill Major Bronston more than you want to find Father," Ruth accused. Slocum wasn't going to gainsay her on this point. It was true. She could offer him all the money in the world, and he'd turn it down just to get even with the Union officer.

"We'll find him. Devils Tower can't be that hard to locate, although I've never been there. It's somewhere outside of Sundance." Slocum finished his beans, and licked the sauce out of the can. Then he tossed it into the pit where Ruth had tried to start a fire. He would bury everything after breakfast to keep any stray Ute off their trail.

"I want to thank you for all you're doing, revenge or not," she said. She shivered as a cold gust of wind blasted down from the high country. Ruth pulled a blanket around her shoulders but shivered again.

"It'll get cold tonight," Slocum said. "We'd best share a blanket."

"For warmth?" she asked, her brown eyes were dancing now. "That is a good idea." Ruth moved closer. Slocum pulled the corner of her blanket over them and they lay back on his. She let out a small sigh and snuggled close to him.

"See, this is better," he said.

"Yes, something is getting quite warm," she said, moving even closer. Her hand worked up and down the inside of his leg and stopped at his crotch. She squeezed gently and felt the throbbing there. Slocum groaned softly as the brunette started kneading what she found there like a mound of dough.

"Enough of that," she said suddenly.

Slocum gasped when her nimble fingers succeeded in unbuttoning his fly. She teased his manhood out and caught it in a firm grip. Moving up and down slowly, she made him so hard he thought he was going to explode like a stick of dynamite.

"That feels mighty good," he said, "but it can get *real* cold."

"Are you saying it might need more shelter than I'm giving?" Ruth's eyes were bright, and a soft flush rose on her neck. She wiggled around so he could hike her skirts and get her undergarments pulled down.

His probing fingers found softness, dampness, and desire. Ruth moaned softly and parted her legs for him.

"You've found all the shelter I can give," she said as her arms went around Slocum's neck and pulled him closer. They kissed as Slocum moved into position with Ruth guiding him eagerly.

Slocum shifted his weight slowly, moving forward until his engorged tip touched her nether lips. Ruth shivered like a leaf in a high wind. Slocum moved a fraction of an inch farther, touching the dampness and warmth that surged up into his loins. He couldn't restrain himself, as much as he wanted to.

He slid balls-deep into the woman's yearning interior. Completely surrounded, he stopped and savored the glow growing within him.

"Move, John, don't stop. Don't stop!" Ruth Waddell sobbed out. Her fingers clawed at his back as her passion grew. Her hips bucked off the hard ground and rotated in an effort to make him sink even deeper.

Slocum pulled back but quickly thrust again. He fell into the rhythm that aroused them both the most. Ruth spurred him on and he couldn't stop, short of being pulled away by wild horses.

"I never thought I'd find someone like you, John," Ruth said, gasping harshly. "You're so good to me—for me!" She shuddered again and arched her back to meet his inward plunge. Slocum gulped when it felt as if a velvet-lined glove had clasped around him.

She squeezed down on his hidden length in ways he had seldom experienced. When her legs wrapped around his waist and her heels locked behind his back, he knew he couldn't get away, even if he wanted. He picked up the pace, friction burning at him. Slocum felt the world begin to spin in wild, crazy circles around him, and he knew he was close.

"Can't hold back," he muttered. "Want to make this last all night, but I can't hold back."

"Don't, don't. Let yourself go," Ruth urged.

Slocum exploded in a white-hot rush. Ruth quaked under him, her voice taken away by the flood of intense desire wracking her. They melted together, then flowed apart laying in each other's arms.

"Sorry," Slocum said. "I hadn't wanted to rush it like that. You have a way about you that does things to me," he said honestly.

"Don't be sorry. I enjoyed it." Ruth fell silent for a long

time, then said, "The night might be very, very long."

"It might be," Slocum answered.

"Good," she said, burrowing under the blankets. Before dawn, it was long several times, and neither one of them complained.

10

Slocum rode a mile ahead of Ruth, who led their spare horses and pack mule. The winding trail through the mountain pass looked clean, but Slocum saw evidence of the Ute war party whenever he dropped to the ground and carefully looked for their spoor. Only occasional horse droppings betrayed them. This told him the Indians were running from someone rather than being on their way to any place in particular.

That made him even warier. The Utes would be riding with one eye on their backs, waiting for the cavalry, or the Arapaho, or whoever to catch up with them.

Midday Slocum camped and let Ruth catch up with him. He saw her riding slowly with her head craning around as if she could detect any Indian laying in ambush. But he didn't laugh at her. She was trying as hard as she could, and better trackers than Slocum had fallen prey to clever traps.

He waved to her and she rode over, leading the mule and horses. Then she dismounted and walked to him, rubbing her behind.

"Well?" she demanded. "What of the Indian braves?"

"They've already hightailed it on through the pass. Whoever's after them isn't in sight yet. We seem to be traveling in the eye of a storm." Slocum pulled the supplies off the mule to give the valiant pack animal a rest. For the first time in over a day he felt easy about making a cook fire, even if he did look for dry wood to hold down the smoke. The meal wasn't much, but it was hot and went down easy.

"So?" Ruth pressed. "What are we going to do?"

"We're going through the pass and ought to be in Cheyenne before sundown. Then, well, we'll have to see if Bronston has beaten us there."

"And if Father is there? What do we do about that?" She hunkered down and ate the food Slocum had fixed greedily. He wasn't much of a cook, but he was better at cooking over a campfire than she was. Slocum wondered about the woman's education. Manners, Latin, and reading all those highfalutin books were fine in New York, but what real good were they? Ruth didn't seem able to think through the practical problems facing them.

"We get to him first, and if we don't, we try to mend fences the best we can," Slocum said. "There's not much to worry our heads over. We either beat Bronston or we don't. This will determine what we do next." He finished and began scraping the debris into the virtually smokeless fire.

"You are taking this much too nonchalantly," she accused. "My father's life is at stake, and you don't seem to care."

"I care," Slocum said. "But I reckon we take care of one problem at a time. Reaching Cheyenne is our first one. If he's gone on to Devils Tower, then so do we. But why worry about the trip to Devils Tower until we need to?" He sprawled on the ground and tipped his broad-brimmed Stetson down to protect his eyes. Slocum needed a nap and this seemed a good time to take one.

"John!" Ruth Waddell was outraged at his inability to worry about the things gnawing at her guts. She sat down hard next to him and glared. Slocum was aware of her angry stare for almost a minute before he drifted off to sleep.

He came awake an hour later, his hand working toward his six-shooter. Slocum shook himself and got up, wondering what had disturbed him. Then it hit him. Ruth wasn't in camp.

Drawing his six-gun, Slocum dropped to one knee and studied the dirt. He found her tracks leading off toward the pass. He counted horses. She had gone on foot. This worried him more than anything else. He had left her in a fine snit, and he'd half expected her to do something stupid. Her walking off like this meant she'd left without a clear plan of action—and she might land herself in a whale of a load of trouble.

Slocum followed the trail, making as much speed as he could without being too careless. He stopped and stared when he found Ruth down by a small stream. She had washed her clothes and maybe taken a bath, but she wasn't paying much attention to her ablutions. She just sat and stared at a square piece of metal.

"You all right?" he asked as his sharp green eyes scanned the rocks around them for any hint of a trap. Ruth Waddell made delectable bait.

"Yes, I'm fine," she said. She held up the metal for him to look at more clearly. A metal frame held a glass plate in place. "This is a photographic plate," she said.

"Can you tell if it was your father's?"

"It was. His initials are scratched on one edge along with a special code number. He was here. This proves it." She looked up, her lovely face drawn with concern.

"Doesn't mean anything happened to him. He just lost a plate, that's all."

"He's always so careful. I've never known him to lose a plate like this." She wiped away a tear.

"I'll look around, but I don't expect to find anything."

"Please look, John." Ruth waited for him to scour the area. He found some evidence that a three-legged stand had been used from shiny, bright metallic scratches on a rock. Other than that, and the photographic plate, there was no evidence that Phillip Waddell had been within a thousand miles of the mountain pass.

"Let's get moving," he said to her, gently helping her up and guiding her back to their camp. They had quite a few miles to go before Cheyenne. Somehow, getting there seemed more important now than ever.

Cheyenne was more to Slocum's liking than Denver. Smaller and more rugged, it had a vitality that made him feel invigorated rather than drained. They rode into town slowly, looking all around for any sign of Bronston or Dickensen. Seeing nothing of the Yankee soldiers, Slocum dismounted and urged Ruth to join him.

"This looks to be the best hotel in town," he said sarcastically while staring at a three-story brick building. The sign was too weathered to read, but he made out OTEL.

"What are you going to do?" she asked.

"I'm going to ask some questions about Bronston. If the train's already pulled in, I don't want him coming up on my blind side when I least expect it."

"I'll register us," she said, giving the hotel a skeptical look.

"Do that. I'll see to the horses when I get back." Slocum settled his gun belt and made sure his Colt Navy rode easily before heading over to the railroad station.

A clerk napped at a desk with his head resting on crossed arms. Slocum looked over the schedule and decided it wouldn't be necessary to wake the snoring man. The train from Denver had arrived that morning. Bronston and Dickensen, if they were on the train, had been in Cheyenne for a goodly eight hours.

Slocum considered stopping at a saloon and wetting his whistle, then he decided against it. He had an obligation to warn Ruth about what he had found concerning the train. Bronston and Dickensen were the bad news no one was ever adequately prepared for.

He walked back to the hotel studying the businesses along Cheyenne's broad main street. He stopped when he saw a photographer's shop. Slocum tried to remember seeing one before and couldn't, but then again, he had never been looking for one. Between saloons, general stores, banks, and undertakers, his business was usually well taken care of.

On impulse, he crossed the street and went into the small shop. Heavy chemical smells made his nostrils twitch. The man behind the counter wore a stiff rubber apron and long gloves dripping with a yellowish fluid that made Slocum want to turn and leave.

"Help you, mister?" the photographer asked. "Don't mind this none. I just got a batch of plates out of the wash."

"The wash?" Slocum wasn't sure if he wanted to know about anything that stunk this bad.

"Developing photo plates." He stripped off the gloves and tossed them onto the counter. Slocum wouldn't have touched them for all the tea in China.

"I was wondering if you happened to talk to another photographer a week or so back," Slocum asked.

The photographer's expression turned neutral, but Slocum was good at reading men. He played poker well, and he knew this man didn't. For all his feigned indifference, he was interested in Slocum's question.

"Can't say one way or the other. Why do you ask?"

"I'm looking for Phillip Waddell. His daughter's hired me to get them together again. She's got a bit of bad news for him—personal news about his wife."

"Do tell," the photographer said, taking off his rubber apron and hanging it behind a small desk. "Seems he's a popular cuss."

"So you have talked to him. And someone else has been asking after him." Slocum's mind raced ahead on the small tidbit the photographer had just tossed out. He wasn't surprised when the man filled in the gaps.

"Two others, a cavalry officer and his sergeant, came by this morning asking after him." The photographer shuddered a little, showing Slocum what he thought of the major.

"What did you tell them?" Slocum tried to keep the edge out of his voice. From the way the photographer jerked around and stared at him, he knew he hadn't quite done it.

"That Waddell was going up toward Devils Tower. Leastwise, that's what he told me ten days ago when he came by. Showed me some of his work, he did. Quite good."

An idea came to Slocum. "Can you develop a photograph Waddell took?" Slocum was thinking of the plate Ruth had found on their way to Cheyenne. It might give some clue as to what the man was doing and perhaps even tell why Bronston wanted to find him.

"Reckon so," the photographer said. "The process isn't that complicated, though it looks like it to those who don't know. See, back in 1851 a limey by the name of Frederick Scott-Archer invented the wet collodion plate process, which must be what you've got."

"What's that?" Slocum asked, not sure he wanted to know.

The photographer smiled and said, "That's a negative which gives unlimited copies. The old daguerreotype method only made one photograph from each exposure."

"Would this cost very much?" Slocum still had a sizable wad of bills riding in his pocket, but he didn't want to squander it. He had been buffaloed and kidnapped before getting it off Michaels and he deserved to keep as much of it as he could for his trouble.

"Not much," the photographer said. "A *carte-de-visite* wet plate is cheap. If you've got the standard 2¼ x 3½ inch plate, I'll print it for you for. . . ." The photographer eyed Slocum, trying to weigh his bankroll. "I'll do it for two dollars."

Slocum didn't know if this was cheap or expensive, but he did know he wanted to see Waddell's photograph. Slocum nodded, told the photographer he'd be back in a few minutes, and hurried out to fetch the plate from Ruth.

She ran into him as he entered the hotel.

"John! I found someone who knows exactly where Father went!"

"Good," Slocum said. "And I found a photographer who can develop that photograph you found. I'm curious to see what's on it."

Emotions played over Ruth's face. "We're so close," she said. "I miss him so much!"

Slocum didn't bother telling her that Bronston and Dickensen were already on her father's trail. They had probably left Cheyenne by now, and posed no immediate threat.

"Let's get the plate developed, then see this guy who knows your pa's whereabouts." Slocum and Ruth returned to the hotel and went up to their room on the third floor. He was secretly pleased to see she had rented only one room, but he wondered if she had lied to the room clerk. The only unmarried women who slept with men were whores.

Slocum tipped his hat in the clerk's direction as they left with the photographic plate, but the man didn't even look up from his work. Slocum relaxed a little, thinking everything was under control. They went to the photographer and gave him the plate. He held it up and examined it for cracks.

"Looks to be in one piece. This will take—"

"An hour," Ruth said. "I am familiar with the process."

"You must be Phillip Waddell's daughter; the one he mentioned." The photographer gestured vaguely in Slocum's direction. From his expression he must have thought Slocum was lying about Ruth's relationship.

"I am, sir."

"I'll get right on this," the photographer promised.

"Good. We have other business to tend to. We'll return in an hour," Slocum said as he steered Ruth from the small shop. The sun had dipped down and the cold evening wind whipped down the street. It wouldn't be long before the saloons got to roaring and the rest of the town went to bed.

"We can find out everything we need, John," Ruth gushed, foolishly optimistic. "I never thought of getting the plate developed. I'm so happy you're with me." She hung on his arm and squeezed.

"I want to talk to this gent you found. Why does he know where your father went?"

"He used to be a scout," Ruth said. "Father went to him for advice."

Slocum followed Ruth to a small store two doors down from the hotel. Sitting in a chair on the walk was a grizzled old man who was whittling on a chunk of pine. He looked up with bleary eyes, spat, and went back to whittling.

"Evening," Slocum said, sitting down. "I understand you spoke with Phillip Waddell about Devils Tower."

"Waddell? Waddell?" The old man tipped his head and peered at Slocum, liking what he saw and deciding to answer. "Yeah, him. The fella with the camera." The cackle the old geezer emitted didn't set well with Slocum.

"Heard tell you were about the best scout in all Wyoming," Slocum went on. "You must have sent Waddell straight to the best place for taking his pictures."

"Just to the south of the tower. Wonderful meadow. Real purty place. Waddell liked the sound of it, he did. Can't get there."

"What? Why not?" Slocum looked at the old man.

"Injuns. Everywhere. Lakota. Arapaho. Wars raging. Fought 'em over the buffalo. Then I was only a little tyke, but I showed 'em all!"

Slocum put his hand on Ruth's arm and pulled her aside, talking to her in a low voice. "I'm not so sure he's reliable," he said. "You keep talking to him and get what you can."

"What are you going to do?"

"I'll check on the photographer. I want to see the picture your pa took."

Slocum returned to the photographer's shop and waited impatiently for the man to emerge from his darkroom. When he finally did, he held up the print, which Slocum grabbed eagerly. Slocum wasn't sure what he expected. All that appeared on the photograph was a tall, rugged butte with clouds giving it a fluffy crown.

"That's it," the photographer said, seeing Slocum's disappointment at the simple picture. "Waddell said he wanted scenery for his book. That's a good shot, nice composition, just a bit off on the exposure, but I can correct for it."

"Thanks," Slocum said, giving the man two greenbacks in payment.

He was disappointed; he didn't know what he had expected to see in Waddell's photograph. He looked up and down Cheyenne's main street and knew something had to break. Bronston wasn't too far ahead, but he might still reach Waddell before Slocum and Ruth did.

Slocum wondered if the old man's senile meandering about a meadow to the south of Devils Tower had any fact to it.

Slocum returned to the store where Ruth was still talking with the old man.

"And then I was ambushed and scalped!" the old man declared. Ruth looked up helplessly. She couldn't sort out the truth from the cobwebs in the old man's worn out brain.

"Do you think he's right about your father heading for this meadow?" Slocum asked.

Ruth shrugged and shook her head. There was no easy answer for that. Slocum thrust his thumbs into his gun belt and leaned against a post, thinking hard. He came to a decision.

"We have to move fast, real fast," he said. "Bronston and his men aren't more than ten hours ahead of us. I can make that time up by noon tomorrow if I ride all night."

"But I never could. . . ." Ruth's words trailed off. She understood what Slocum was saying. "No!" she flared. "I will *not* stand by idly while my father is in such danger."

"You don't even know what Bronston wants from him," Slocum pointed out. He touched the empty watch pocket on his vest and knew precisely what he wanted from Bronston. "If I stop Bronston and Dickensen, then there'll be all the time in the world to find your father."

"No."

"You have to find somebody in town who knows exactly where your pa headed," Slocum said. "The photographer might know more than he told me. He gets loose-jawed if you ask him about his damned pictures. You can talk to him. And this old coot might actually know something, or someone else in town might. It's too late now to find them." Slocum readied more arguments but they weren't needed.

"You've made your point. Truth to tell, a rest would do me some good," Ruth said, rubbing her bottom. She smiled wanly and asked, "Can you stop Major Bronston?"

"I've got to catch up with him first," Slocum said. But he knew he could overtake Bronston, especially if surprise was in his favor. He had a new rifle, ammo for it, and he could get fresh horses. The odds rode with him this time.

"Go find him, John. For me." Ruth gave him a quick kiss and turned away. He thought tears were forming in her eyes, but he wasn't going to check to be sure. She wanted to play a major part in finding her father, and she was upset that she was unable to do so.

Slocum got his horses, packed his supplies, checked his rifle, and started out. It would be a long, hard ride at night through unknown country, but a full moon would give him an edge in tracking Bronston and his men.

11

Slocum wobbled in the saddle from lack of sleep. He had ridden hard all night following what he hoped was Bronston's trail. He had worked along a fan-shaped path, going back and forth until he came upon a recent trail going north toward Chugwater Creek. Cheyenne was a busy town, but the number of people coming or going in any day, even north toward Fort Laramie, told Slocum a group of five riders was unusual.

In the brightness of the full moon he followed the trail until he was sure it had to be Bronston. As if the Yankee major had lined up on the polestar, the tight group of riders headed straight north. When he had decided to commit totally to this spoor, Slocum had ridden for all he was worth.

An hour's ride on one horse tired it enough to force him to switch to the spare. Hour after hour Slocum rode at a pace that could cover fifty miles in a day. Just after sunup, he slowed to reconnoiter. Slocum didn't want to blunder onto Bronston's camp.

He dismounted and studied the ground for more sign's of recent passage. He found a shod hoofprint or two in the soft dirt that encouraged him, but Slocum went cold inside when he saw other spoor.

"Ute," he muttered to himself. A dozen unshod ponies, maybe more, had passed along this section of trail. He tried to put a time on it and he couldn't. His best guess was that the Indian war party had gone to the north hours before Bronston had ridden the same trail.

Bronston was following the Indians and didn't know it, Slocum suspected.

If there was any justice, the Utes would ambush the officer, Dickensen, and the other three with them. But Slocum knew there was only one type of surefire justice. His hand touched the ebony handle of his Colt Navy.

It was the justice he made for himself.

Slocum wanted to push on immediately, but he held back long enough to chew on some jerky. Pushing himself to the limit would be foolhardy if he had to confront Bronston, but facing the man wasn't what he intended. Slocum wanted his watch back with the least possible trouble. Killing Bronston seemed the best way to do that.

Slocum smiled crookedly. Killing Bronston had another benefit. It kept the officer away from Phillip Waddell. Everything would be tied up in one neat package. One bullet, one solution to two problems. Slocum liked the way everything fell into place.

He switched mounts again and started out at a trot, this time not pushing as hard as he had all night, but he was still making good time. He kept a sharp eye on the ground and saw the signs of passage increase. Luck sided with Slocum when he heard the distant neighing of a horse before he saw Bronston's camp.

He dismounted and tied his two horses securely to a scrub oak. Slocum checked the new rifle he had bought in Cheyenne, worrying that he hadn't taken time to sight it in properly. He decided this wouldn't matter if he got close enough for the shot he wanted. He levered a round into the chamber and added a spare cartridge to the magazine, then Slocum set off to find his prey.

Slocum walked slowly, making sure of each step. The crack of a dried twig or the crunch of gravel under his boots might give him away. He dived flat on his belly when he suddenly saw the silhouette of a sentry against the dawn sky. Glad for his caution, Slocum lay still several minutes and just observed.

Two guards were posted high in the rocks, almost a quarter of the way up the side of a canyon. From that position they commanded a view of the trail in either direction. But Slocum saw their mistake; if he stayed close to the rocky face of the stone cliff, they wouldn't see him, or be able to fire on him without exposing their position.

He crept closer to the stone cliff and pressed his back against it. Several times Slocum looked up to be sure he was right. He heard the sentries moving about, but he couldn't see them. A slow smile crossed his face. Bronston might be a military man, but he knew little about posting guards. The cavalry insignia on his uniform jacket might mean he was more at home on the plains than in the mountains. That suited Slocum just fine because it meant Bronston's death.

A low rise separated Slocum from the camp. He heard voices and smelled a campfire. Its pungent scent of burning juniper mixed with the aroma of fresh coffee drifted toward him. With his mouth watering, Slocum moved closer. A final quick look up convinced him the guards were not in any position to see him.

"Reckon it's about time I invited myself to breakfast," Slocum said softly to himself as he stretched out on the rocky slope. He studied the camp below and again saw evidence of Bronston's military training. The horses were penned some distance away. If shooting started, they might not be hit. On the other hand, a Ute could sneak into the simple corral and steal the horses.

Slocum paused as he considered this. Bronston was no fool. He would never put his horses in such jeopardy for the slight benefit of keeping the animals away from the camp. Then he figured it out. Both sentries had a clear shot at the flat land around the corral. The guards *did* watch over the horses.

That made Slocum feel a mite better. Bronston was no fool, and anything that seemed foolish had to be a trap. Bronston had gone by the book and wouldn't expect what Slocum had come to deliver.

The three in the camp were crouched by the camp fire. It was just past sunup, but Slocum couldn't make out who the dark figures were. One had to be Bronston, another Dickensen, and the third a henchman. But who was who? Slocum wanted the head, not the body, of this beast.

He sighted at a point in the center of the three, ready to shift quickly when Bronston revealed himself. The men drank their coffee and talked in low whispers.

"Hey, Major!" came a loud shout from above.

Slocum shrank down, lowering his rifle and trying not to be seen by either of the sentries in the rocks.

All three men looked up, not giving Slocum any clue as to which one of them was Bronston.

"Major, when can we come on down? It's getting cold up here."

"Shut your damned mouth, Abbot," snapped Dickensen. "You will direct any complaints to me, not the major. And you've got another hour of sentry duty."

"Aw, Sarge, we're both gettin' powerful hungry," protested the sentry. Slocum knew this wasn't the Army, or

Dickensen would have ordered Abbot flogged for insubordination. But the exchange did eliminate one of the three at the campfire.

He knew which was Dickensen.

That left two. Slocum considered his chances of plugging both the other men, but they didn't look good. He tried to guess which one of them was about Bronston's size, then he centered his sights on the man's back, but still he waited some more. He had come too far to rush it. During the war he had been a sniper, and patience had been his greatest weapon. He was a good shot, but he had always waited for the best chance at hitting his target before firing.

Slocum seldom missed because of his being so picky.

The one he thought was Bronston stood and turned to Dickensen. The two exchanged a few words and Slocum knew he had been right. He had correctly chosen. His finger drew back for the killing shot, but he paused just before the round was triggered.

"Why?" he muttered to himself. Why was Bronston so persistent in hunting down Phillip Waddell? Ruth didn't know. Slocum had thought she might be hiding something, but that impression had vanished as he got to know her better. She was a terrible liar, and when she said she didn't know any Major Bronston, Slocum had to believe her.

His curiosity rose and Slocum wanted answers, but he wasn't going to let this get in his way. He could make the shot and get away scot-free, but still he hesitated.

Bronston made a gesture of dismissal and sent Dickensen back to the campfire. Then the major turned and walked downhill from the camp, vanishing behind a boulder. Slocum considered what the man was up to, then smiled. He might be able to get his watch back without firing a shot *and* get a tad of information in the bargain.

Sliding backward, Slocum got his feet under him and duck walked around the rise. He was conscious of the two men in the rocks above him, but he doubted they would notice movement this close to camp. They were cold, tired, and hungry, and wouldn't be too sharp. Also, Slocum figured Bronston had posted them to watch the trail as well as the horses. They'd be more interested in anyone approaching the camp along the trail than in any movement directly below them.

At least, that's what Slocum hoped.

He went quickly, rounding the low rise and coming out on the far side of the boulder where Bronston had vanished. Slocum kept low and used his hearing more than his eyes. The major was on the far side of a bush, relieving himself.

Slocum knew he'd never have a better opportunity. He rounded the boulder, located the major who stood with his back to him, and moved fast.

He shoved the Winchester's barrel up hard against Bronston's back while the man was still pissing.

"You got some questions to answer," Slocum said.

"What?" Bronston tried to turn. Slocum swung the barrel and rapped him smartly on the side of the head. Bronston recoiled and almost fell to his knees.

"Why are you after Phillip Waddell?"

"Who the hell are you?" demanded Bronston. "I thought you were some saddle bum the girl had hired, but you're too persistent."

"Why are you after Waddell?" Slocum repeated. "And where's my watch?"

"That's what this is all about? I got your damned watch and you're going to back shoot me?" Bronston laughed harshly.

"Answer the question," Slocum said, growing wary. Bronston was playing for time. Dickensen might follow his commander downhill, or one of the sentries up in the mountainside might spot something out of the ordinary. Slocum checked to be sure the huge boulder blocked the direct view from above. He was exposed—but not as exposed as Bronston.

"Keep that in your hand. That way I know what you're doing," Slocum ordered. He reached around and grabbed the handle of Bronston's pistol. He jerked it free and stuck it into his own belt. Slocum didn't want a spare six-shooter laying around where Bronston might get lucky and pick it up again.

"If I give you the watch, will that be the end of it?" asked Bronston.

"Not now," said Slocum. "You had me beat up and kidnapped. You've got too much to answer for."

"The authorities?" Bronston laughed harshly. "They are fools. They tried to—"

The major ducked under the barrel of Slocum's rifle and tried to turn and grapple with him. Slocum stepped back, brought the stock of the Winchester up, and clipped Bronston under the chin. The Yankee officer stiffened, his eyes rolled up in his head, and then he pitched face down into the dirt.

Slocum might not get any answers from the unconscious Bronston, but he'd get his watch—and satisfaction.

12

Slocum stepped back, wiped the sweat from his forehead, then poked Bronston's ribs with the rifle muzzle. The Yankee officer didn't stir. Slocum rested the Winchester against a rock, grabbed Bronston's arm, and rolled the man onto his back. For a moment Slocum just stared at him.

He had never gotten a close look at Bronston's uniform before. Slocum frowned as he ran his fingers over the torn spots on the front of it and on the arms, places where insignia had once been sewn. The buttons had been sewn back onto the uniform with a different thread, and all hint of braid had been ripped off.

"I'll be damned," Slocum said, slowly realizing what the rips meant. Bronston had been cashiered from the Union Army. All insignia, medals, and decoration had been removed forcibly. Bronston had replaced only the buttons and major's leaves.

Slocum reached over and drew the saber. It was whole, but he could picture a general officer taking Bronston's saber and breaking it over his knee. Whatever the major had done, it had been significant enough to get him court-martialed and kicked out of the cavalry. It might even have been enough to get him thrown into the Detroit Penitentiary, as the marshal back in Dodge City had mentioned.

Slocum replaced the saber, then opened the buttons to Bronston's jacket and fished around inside of it for the watch. He smiled when his fingers found the slick metal case and the heavy gold chain attached to it. Before he could pull it free, a strong hand clamped on his wrist and twisted it hard.

He grunted in pain and tried to break free. He did, but his leverage was wrong. Slocum went tumbling and fetched up hard against a rock.

Bronston struggled to his feet, his thin face a mask of fury. "You can't do that, you Southern son of a bitch. I spit on men like you. I *enjoy* spitting on you!"

Slocum kicked out and caught Bronston behind the left knee. The Yankee officer toppled, but he had regained his senses fully. He twisted lithely and scuttled away on both hands and his good leg. Slocum saw Bronston getting away and knew what had to be done.

He went for his Colt and cocked it.

Bronston started shouting for help from his camp. Slocum couldn't allow him to go on for long or Dickensen and the other three would be down on him in a flash. Slocum got off a shot, but Bronston was ducking and dodging too fast to ever be hit with a wild round.

With his own feet under him again, Slocum took off after Bronston, only to skid to a halt and saw the pair of guards straining to figure out what was going on. One called down to his sergeant. Slocum couldn't hear Dickensen's reply, but he imagined it had to be, "Shoot anything that moves."

As if they were reading his mind, a bullet kicked up a tiny cloud of dust not five feet away. Slocum dashed back for the cover afforded by the boulder. Going after Bronston was out of the question unless he got rid of the guards positioned high in the mountainside. And Slocum didn't think he could outrun the man, not the way he'd hightailed it.

There had to be a better plan.

Slocum thought hard for several seconds, then a smile curled his lips. He couldn't go after Bronston without getting ventilated, but he could try to spook the others.

Slocum circled the boulder, keeping the rock between him and the snipers. Then he started making war whoops, shouting words of Ute, Crow, Apache, and any other Indian lingo he had picked up in the past, while shooting into the camp.

Dickensen swung around and opened fire with his pistol. The other man grabbed a military carbine and shot wildly; he did not have a good target. This momentary confusion gave Slocum time to reload and turn his attention to the men higher on the cliff. Leveling his rifle, he waited for the right moment. And it came, as he knew it would.

One guard poked his head out to see what the ruckus was all about. Slocum squeezed off the shot. The man's hat blew off into thin air and his head vanished—but Slocum felt good about the shot. He had hit the man square between the eyes.

"Sarge, Sarge, Joe's dead! He got it right smack-dab in the face!"

"Shut up!" bellowed Dickensen. "Get a bead on them Injuns."

"Indians!" The man in camp with Dickensen turned in surprise. "We're fighting goddamn Indians?"

Slocum let out another whoop and followed it with five quick shots. The lead stirred a bedroll and spooked the horses, but did no real damage. It didn't matter because he had completely demoralized Bronston's men. Only Dickensen kept his head, and maybe he would get it blown off if the other two panicked enough.

He reloaded and turned his attention to the lone sniper on the cliff face. Slocum got off a couple shots, then started moving back to where he had ambushed Bronston. He doubted the guard up in the cliffs was going to pay much attention to a white man moving around if he thought Indians were after his scalp.

Slocum dashed after Bronston, then figured out that the man would try to circle and come into the camp from the far side, near the corral of horses. This afforded him the maximum cover and the least chance of being potshot along the way. This was fine with Slocum. He didn't want Bronston heading straight back into the camp. He would be able to cut the cavalry officer off and keep him from both camp and horse. Keeping low, Slocum cut diagonally across the narrow valley, then began to circle back in toward Dickensen and the others.

He knelt and studied the cliff for any sign of the rifleman. He almost laughed when he saw the man tumbling down the rocky face. Bronston's one ace had just been taken out of the deck. With Dickensen and the other two in the camp, they would never be able to get a decent shot at him before he captured Bronston.

A few more war whoops cut through the still morning air, echoing down the canyon until they faded entirely. Slocum knew that this would hold the men in the camp as if he had stuck their feet in glue. Faster now, he raced for the far side of the corral, keeping a screen of lodgepole pines between him and the campsite.

Slocum dropped to his knees and waited, trying to still his own harsh breathing. He heard faint sounds of movement farther toward the distant canyon wall. He had made it around in time to intercept Bronston!

Stirring noises came from the direction of the camp. Slocum cursed the speed with which Dickensen had whipped his men into action. He turned and got off a shot at the sergeant. The lead whined past Dickensen's ear and drove him to cover. The other man bolted and ran, not caring about returning fire.

"That ought to keep you busy for just long enough," Slocum said to himself. He turned back to the task of locating the approaching Major Bronston.

Working his way outward, Slocum found a niche between two fallen trees. He wedged himself in and swung his rifle around, resting it in a convenient V formed by a rotting trunk and a limb. He calmed himself, and practiced the shot over and over. When Bronston actually showed, Slocum had killed the man a dozen times over.

The trigger came back smoothly but the bullet didn't fly true. Slocum cursed, levered a new round into the chamber, and tried for a second shot—but it was too late. Bronston wrenched himself to one side and dived into a thicket, making a clean shot impossible.

Aware that Dickensen and the other two might show up behind him at any moment, Slocum raced forward. He wanted to know why Bronston was tracking down Phillip Waddell, but even more he wanted his watch back. Taking it off a dead man didn't bother him much.

Slocum charged pell-mell, not caring if he got scratched up in the thicket protecting Bronston. He shoved the brambles out of the way with the butt of his rifle, but the major was nowhere to be seen. Slocum cocked his head to one side, listening intently. Bronston couldn't have gone far. If he was close, Slocum would be able to hear him breathing hard, and if he was running, Slocum would be able to hear his feet pounding.

His sixth sense warned him of the attack just in time. Slocum dropped to one knee, twisted around, and swung the rifle muzzle toward his rear. He fired at the dark object hurtling down from above and saw a shower of blood and fabric as he wounded Bronston.

Then the major hit him hard and sent him rolling. Slocum tried to hang onto the rifle but couldn't. Rocks and brambles cut his hands. He came to his feet and saw Bronston reaching for the rifle.

Slocum's hand went for the major's six-shooter stuck in his belt. Slocum drew and fired five times. One bullet hit the rifle and caused it to spin away in a shower of sparks, the others missed. Even if Bronston reached the Winchester, it wasn't likely to be in operating condition.

"The last round is for you," Slocum said. He pulled the trigger and the hammer fell on an empty cylinder.

Again Bronston judged the situation properly. He attacked, drawing his cavalry saber and swinging it over his head. If he had tried running away, Slocum would have gone for his Colt Navy and drilled him in the back.

Grappling with the former Union officer, Slocum grabbed his uplifted wrist and tried to force the saber from Bronston's grip. They rolled over and over on the ground until Bronston came out on top.

Bronston couldn't force the saber closer to Slocum, and he couldn't escape, but it finally came to him that he had allies not far away.

"Dickensen! Here! I've got him over here!"

Slocum reared up and smashed his forehead into Bronston's mouth. A geyser of blood flowed from the man's split lip. Best of all, Slocum had silenced the shouts for aid. The pain caused Bronston to pull back just enough for Slocum to gain the upper hand. He pulled free and slammed his right hand hard into Bronston's face.

The officer crumpled, giving Slocum the chance to get to his feet. He went for his Colt only to be slammed forward hard. He staggered and sank to one knee, shaking his head.

Reaching back, his fingers found the spot where a bullet had grazed his back.

Through blurry eyes, he saw Dickensen lifting his pistol for a second shot. Slocum fired twice in the sergeant's direction. This was enough to drive him to cover—and to give Bronston the diversion he needed to get away again.

"My watch. Dammit, he has my brother's watch," Slocum told himself. Anger replaced the weakness flooding his body. His lips pulled back into a thin line and Slocum stumbled after the fleeing major. If he had to fight every cavalry officer in the Union to get the watch back he'd do it. All through the war he had done it and lived.

He'd do it again, and win.

Ahead he heard heavy crashing through the underbrush. Slocum homed in on it like an eagle going for a rabbit in a meadow. Blood blinded one eye and his head pounded fiercely from the grazing he had taken from Dickensen's bullet, but he kept going. People had always called him stubborn, now Slocum was going to prove it.

The blue of Bronston's uniform flickered through the green of the dense brush just ahead. Slocum fired and missed. He saw Bronston veer to the right, trying to make a wider circle that would get him back to the camp. Not only were his allies there, but Bronston could also get another weapon. Slocum had to keep him from rifles and six-shooters.

Cutting parallel to Bronston's path, Slocum plunged through the dense growth. From behind him he heard wild whoops like he had made to spook Dickensen and the others. He wondered why the sergeant would try to decoy him away with the trick Slocum had already used effectively. Not thinking straight, Slocum kept moving, fighting to put one foot in front of the other.

He saw Bronston enter a small clearing. He fired at the man and Bronston dived flat to avoid being ventilated. Slocum ran after him, more intent on the officer than where he was putting his feet. Slocum stepped into a shallow trench, got his foot tangled in a vine, and went down heavily.

When he tried to get up, he found himself inextricably tangled. Cursing, he fought to get free. Then he froze.

"Aieee!"

The war cry echoed across the clearing and caused Bronston to poke his head up for a look. Slocum saw their mutual danger about the same time the officer did.

Slocum had faked his Indian war cries, but these weren't from any pretender. Three Ute braves waving war lances and rifles ran into the clearing intent on capturing Bronston.

Finally jerking his foot free, Slocum lifted his six-gun to kill the Indians. His finger froze on the trigger. Four more braves joined the three moving in on Bronston. Before he could take another breath, they were joined by two more.

Nine Ute warriors poked and prodded at Bronston and there was nothing Slocum could do about it. He watched helplessly as the source of the answers to his questions was herded away.

And with Bronston went Slocum's watch.

13

John Slocum rubbed his turned ankle, fuming at the way fate had betrayed him. He had almost caught Bronston fair and square, yet the major was beyond his reach. Slocum snorted in disgust at the thought that his ploy of faking a Ute attack on Bronston's camp had brought down the actual raiding party.

He took the time to reload his Colt Navy, both Bronston's pistol and the rifle had been lost in the pines. Slocum got to his feet and gingerly took a step. His ankle supported his weight; it seemed he hadn't done too much damage to himself, and the fall might have saved his life. The Ute had missed him and gone straight for the major.

Slocum didn't fool himself on that score. The Indians had seen a uniformed enemy and wanted him for torture. If they had found any other white man, they would have killed him outright. Slocum didn't know what had been going on to stir up the Indians, but it had to be something the cavalry had done. Shaking his head, he made his way across the clearing, going in the direction taken by the Utes.

The U.S. Cavalry had a terrible record of keeping down the Indians. More likely than not, they'd massacre a village of women and children rather than face a real battle with warriors. Such tactics had worked for de Anza when he fought the Comanche, but the Utes, Crow, and Sioux were not the enemy-eating rulers of the Staked Plains. Different tactics were needed to bring them to bay.

If an officer fell into their hands, and enough atrocities had been heaped on their heads, there was no telling what they'd do.

"My watch," Slocum complained. "I want my watch back, and now I have to save that bastard's worthless hide." He dropped to one knee and studied the tracks. The Utes walked light, leaving only a few bent blades of grass. Bronston's path was more pronounced. Heavy boot heels dug in here and there, showing where the cavalry officer had tried to fight his captors.

Slocum started on the trail, but then slowed and halted. He heard sounds behind him. He edged around a tall pine and pressed his back into it. He wondered if his luck would ever change for the better. Dickensen and his remaining man were on the same trail.

"Dammit, Major, where are you?" shouted Dickensen.

"I tell you they was Injuns," the other man said fearfully. "We can't go up agin' a whole damn war party."

"Shut up," Dickensen snapped. "There weren't any Indians. That was a trick, and you fell for it. Somebody's grabbed the major, and we've got to rescue him."

"Utes, I tell you," said the other man. "I know them. I lived in these parts for a year or two. They've been ranging farther and farther each year. Mostly they was keepin' down in southern Colorado, but no more."

"I don't give two hoots what you think," Dickensen said. "I'll shoot you for insubordination if you don't get moving."

Slocum considered letting out a war whoop or two to give Dickensen some incentive for turning tail and running. He kept quiet knowing such a trick could bring down the Utes. The Indians might take care of the men on Slocum's trail, but they might also have a chance to put an arrow through his chest.

"Lookee here," said the soldier. "This here's an Indian feather. They wear 'em when they're in a war party."

Slocum didn't chance a glance back. A Ute warrior must have lost some decoration. He tried to figure out what to do. There didn't seem to be any point in letting Dickensen follow the Utes and get massacred. If anything, this would put the Indians on guard and make rescuing Bronston—and Slocum's watch—all the more difficult.

He crouched down and made his way to the north at a right angle to the trail taken by the Indians and their captive. Slocum made just enough noise to arouse Dickensen's attention.

"There, something's going off in that direction."

"Injuns!"

"No, you fool. Somebody's after the major. You saw him yourself. He's the one who plugged Joe and tried to kill you. It's a white man, not some troop of Indians," insisted Dickensen.

Slocum kept moving slowly to draw them into following, then he moved faster. He didn't care if he made noise since it would draw them like flies to a decaying carcass. Then Slocum suddenly changed direction and laid low, waiting to see if his decoying tactics worked.

They did. Dickensen and the man with him passed within two yards of his hiding place without seeing him as they hurried on a wild-goose chase.

Slocum worried they had found his two horses, but he would have to deal with that problem later. If his luck turned, he might be able to steal a Ute pony, but Slocum shook himself free of making plans like that. He had to roll with the punches and just stay alive for the next few hours. And he had to find Bronston. That rankled him most of all. He'd as soon gut-shoot the son of a bitch as follow him into a Ute war camp to save him.

Finding the trail was difficult but Slocum managed. He walked carefully, making as little noise as possible in the brush area. He didn't know where the Utes had camped, nor did he know if they had slung Bronston over a pony and ridden off. If so, he might never be able to recover his watch. Getting back to his horses and finding the Utes' trail was more than he wanted to tackle.

Slocum fell flat on his face when he heard sounds ahead. He lifted his head slowly and peered ahead. Two Utes stood with their arms crossed, barely visible in the shadows. One called to the other, who then replied. Slocum didn't understand enough of their lingo to know what they said, but from the way they laughed it seemed it had to do with Bronston.

Edging forward slowly, he came within a few yards of the two Indians without being seen. He considered removing both Indians. A single shot would take out one, and he could overpower the other, but he quickly pushed such an idea aside. Even a single shot might attract the other Indians in the war party.

He started to circle and get to the east of the two guards when a shout brought them around. They ran lightly into the brush, leaving their guard post untended. Slocum hurried after them, knowing they had been summoned to the torture.

In a small draw he saw the Utes, twenty strong, in a circle around Bronston. They had staked him out on the ground. Slocum couldn't see what they were doing to the man at first, then he understood. The Utes intended to make this a long, painful torture.

They had put rawhide strips around his ankles, wrists, head, and middle, then soaked them in water. The stretched, damp rawhide would dry and contract in the hot sun. Bronston's arms, legs, head, and body would be racked by pain in an hour. By sundown he would be pleading for death, and by then the Utes would have other tortures ready, maybe with knives or fire.

The Utes watched silently as Bronston struggled and shouted curses at them. Their leader pointed, and they left silently. Slocum wished he had his spyglass with him. He needed to know how far away the Indians camped before trying anything.

He let out a pent-up breath when he saw a lone Ute return and sit a few yards from him, intent on watching Bronston's struggles. Slocum guessed the brave had been wronged by the cavalry in some particular fashion, and this was his revenge. The Ute took out his knife and made drawings in the sandy ground occasionally looking up at Bronston.

"You'll burn in hell for this," Bronston promised, struggling against the rawhide strips. "You'll be *lucky* to burn there if I get loose first!"

The threats didn't affect the warrior. He hunkered down and continued making his mystic signs in the sand. Slocum stood up and looked around, wondering if he ought to risk his neck like this. He didn't know if the Ute had searched their prisoner and taken the watch, or if it still rode in Bronston's inner pocket.

There was only one way to find out.

Slocum slipped down the slope behind the Ute, being careful not to make any sound or cast a shadow so the warrior might be warned. With his Colt Navy in hand, Slocum got close enough to make his attack. He reared back just as the Indian turned. The barrel of the six-shooter landed with a sick crunch on the side of the Ute's head.

The Indian collapsed as though he had been poleaxed.

"You don't give up, do you?" snapped Bronston. "Get me free."

"First things first," Slocum said, starting toward the bound man.

"Come any closer and I shout my lungs out. You'll never get away from them. There are too many Indians in that war party for you to believe that."

"They'll kill you," Slocum said, hesitating. He was ten feet from Bronston. He could shoot the major, but the report would bring the Indians running. Slocum looked down at his feet and saw the fallen brave's knife, but he wouldn't be able to get to it before Bronston could start shouting.

"What do I have to lose? Free me."

Slocum hesitated, considering his chances. He could go along with Bronston's order, then use the knife on the man's exposed neck.

"This headband's getting mighty tight," Bronston said, "and I'm getting impatient." He paused for a moment, then asked, "What the hell do you want from me? I don't know you."

"If you don't let me get close to you, how am I supposed to cut you free?"

"Use the knife. I've seen the way you move. That toad sticker's no mystery for you. Throw it and cut the rawhide on my left hand."

"I might miss," Slocum said, bending to pick up the sharp knife. He looked back uphill in the direction taken by the others in the war party. A single toss might solve his problems. Land the knife in Bronston's throat and he wouldn't be able to shout.

Almost as if Bronston had read his mind, the officer tucked his chin down hard against his chest. Making that throw, even if Slocum had been expert enough with the strangely balanced knife, was now out of the question.

"I might miss."

"Try," urged Bronston. "I've put up with worse than a few cuts in that damned Yankee prison."

Slocum blinked at the man's words. He didn't understand exactly what Bronston meant.

"Do it. Now!" Bronston's voice rose. "I'm getting ready to call them back. I don't have any time for your dawdling."

Slocum picked up the Indian's dropped knife and stepped closer until Bronston told him to stop.

"Drive it into my chest and I can still bring them down on your neck. I promise I'll see you scalped before I die!" Again Bronston had stopped him from scheming.

Slocum threw the knife, aiming for the man's face. A knife point through an eye would kill instantly. But the knife hadn't set well in his hand, and his toss was off by several inches. The blade slid into the sand beside Bronston's left arm.

The officer ran the rawhide strip up and down once and cut it through. He snared the knife and quickly freed his right hand and ankles, then he cut the band from his middle. Slocum took another step, thinking he could buffalo Bronston as he had the Indian.

Bronston shook off the rawhide headband and got to his feet.

"You're a stupid son of a bitch," he sneered. "You should have killed me when you had the chance."

"If we head straight back toward your camp, we can lose them. They won't notice you're gone for an hour or two."

"Not until sundown," Bronston said.

Slocum took a quick step in Bronston's direction, hoping to catch the cavalry officer off guard. Slocum was too slow, and his move worked against him, he had misjudged Bronston's resolve. He grabbed Slocum's arm, yanked hard, and sent him reeling. A savage slash with the knife made Slocum feel as though his left hand had almost been separated from his arm as he stumbled past. Blood flowed and pain shot up into his shoulder.

"They don't care who they've got," Bronston sneered. "You'll do just fine." He kicked out, sending Slocum down the bank of a ravine, then he landed squarely on his back. With the air knocked forcefully from his lungs, Slocum lay gasping like a fish out of water.

Through the haze of pain, Slocum heard Bronston hooting and hollering to summon the war party. By the time they would arrive to find their prisoner gone, Bronston would have made his escape—and Slocum would be his replacement.

14

Slocum struggled to get his breath back, but it felt as if his chest had been crushed. He heard Bronston whoop and shout at the Utes one more time, taunting them with the attack on their sentry. Then there was only an ominous silence.

Rolling onto his side sent arrows of pain shooting through Slocum's body, but instead of paralyzing him, it forced him into action. His left arm was bleeding from the cut Bronston had given him, but this would be the least of his worries if the Utes found him. The Ute guard he had slugged wouldn't care if he was a cavalry officer, the torture the war party had decided on for Bronston would be only the beginning if they caught him.

Slocum panted like a dog as he rolled onto his hands and knees. The air returned slowly to his lungs, but it came. He stood and clutched at his bleeding arm. If he didn't take care of it quickly, he'd lose so much blood he'd weaken and be easy prey. Slocum strained to hear sounds of the Indians coming, but he heard nothing.

Awkwardly ripping his shirt sleeve, he bound his wound. A flap of skin had been sliced back. He carefully tucked it under the bandage and pulled as hard as he could, tying it off by using his teeth on the cloth. The cut wasn't as bad as he'd first thought, but it was damned messy. Being trailed by skillful trackers like the Utes required all his wit and ability. It wouldn't do leaving a stream of blood any six-year-old Indian child could find.

Slocum finished his crude patching and looked around to see how bad his position was. He had tumbled down into a dry creek bed. Come early spring, it probably ran full with runoff from melting snow higher in the mountains, but now it was dry.

Slocum got his bearings and started upstream, away from Bronston's camp—and his own horses. Without the horses, Slocum had no chance of escaping, but he dared not go in the same direction as the cavalry officer. The Utes would go that way because Bronston was such a piss-poor woodsman. The best he could hope for was to circle behind the Indians and follow them to Bronston's camp.

Slocum kept listening for the Utes but he never heard them. This made him edgier than if he'd detected the whole band of them on his heels. He had to find the Indians or he'd blunder across them when he least expected it.

The dry creek narrowed and meandered off toward the side of the canyon. Slocum took the chance to clamber from the rocky bed and up onto the bank. He stayed flat, studying the creek bed in both directions to see if he was being followed. He saw and heard nothing. He moved into a stand of pines and flitted from tree to tree until he got back to the sandy draw where the Utes had staked out Bronston.

The Ute he had buffaloed lay still and unmoving. Slocum wondered if he had killed the brave. He tried to remember the feel of the barrel hitting the man's head. There had been a loud crunching sound as if bones might have broken, but nothing to hint that the blow had killed him. Slocum had been so involved with Bronston that he hadn't bothered checking the fallen Ute.

Slocum stayed where he was, playing a waiting game. He saw no reason for the Ute to be acting as a decoy. After five minutes the brave hadn't moved a muscle. Slocum went over to him, knelt, and felt for a pulse in his throat. He had killed the Ute.

Only the soft whistle of wind through the tall pines came to Slocum's ears. Where were the Utes? He couldn't believe they hadn't accepted Bronston's challenge. Letting a prisoner escape was a shortcoming that approached outright sin for them.

Slocum looked up just in time to see the air filled with a diving red-skinned body. He reacted, but it was far too slowly. The Ute slammed hard into him and sent him tumbling onto the sandy ground where Bronston had been tied.

With savage silence, the Ute tried to slice his throat open with a wickedly sharp knife. Slocum held the brave's wrist with his injured left arm and felt himself weakening quickly. The knife's point descended inexorably, now aimed for his chest.

Slocum shouted to focus his strength and managed to get the Ute off him. He wanted to land on top of the warrior, but the Indian knew this trick and used it against him. Slocum ended up under the descending knife once more.

His arm began to bleed sluggishly through his rude bandage, and pain shot through his body. Slocum kicked hard and got his legs up. The Ute made a mistake then. He straightened and this allowed Slocum to wrap his legs around his head. Using all his strength, Slocum heaved and pulled the brave off him. The man fell to one side, grunted, and lay still.

Slocum whipped out his six-shooter and cocked it, ready to shoot. To hell with drawing the others in the war party. But the Indian didn't move.

"What're you trying to do?" Slocum asked. He shoved the Indian and rolled him over. The brave had fallen on his own knife and had died silently.

Slocum wondered why the attack hadn't been accompanied with the usual war cries. The brave's mouth gaped slightly. Slocum looked into the Ute's mouth and saw the answer. At sometime in the past, his tongue had been cut out.

Slocum shuddered at the close call and looked around, worrying that others in the band would come down on him. He stood up and turned when he heard distant gunfire. Slocum checked the fallen Indian one last time to be sure he was dead, picked up the knife that had gutted the Ute, then headed for Bronston's camp.

He went slowly, not sure what he might find. The absolute silence after Bronston's initial shouts spooked him a mite. Slocum paused when he saw evidence of several Utes' passage. Weeds had been trampled, as if the braves hadn't cared who saw their tracks. Slocum knelt and considered what he saw.

More gunfire told of a battle raging in Bronston's camp. The major and his men were no match for the entire war party. That they had camped so close without one knowing of the other's existence was a testament to the way sounds traveled in the uneven canyon. Some sounds were muffled and others magnified.

Slocum came to a quick decision. He retraced the Utes' path, hunting for their camp. The closer he got to it, the more cautious he became. He didn't know how they guarded their precious ponies, or if they would have left anyone behind to stand lookout, but he knew he'd find out soon.

He intended to steal their horses.

His nose alerted him of a campfire before he saw the Utes' small encampment. Slocum went to ground, wiggling forward on his belly until he came to the edge of a small clearing. He frowned when he saw a remuda of horses, but no sentry. Leaving camp to pursue an escaping enemy was one thing, but to run off without posting a lookout wasn't the way any war party worked.

Slocum wasn't sure what warned him. The hair on the back of his neck rose, prompting him to roll over, and bring his Colt Navy up. A war lance batted it out of his hand.

"Aieee!"

The Ute warrior rose above him with his eagle-feathered war lance ready to pin him solidly to the ground. Slocum reacted rather than thought about what to do. He kicked and caught the brave in the knee. The Ute didn't stop his attack, but because of his injured kneecap, his thrust was just enough off target to let Slocum live.

Slocum didn't have the strength to fight the Indian, and his six-shooter was too far for him to grab. He wrenched around, kicked again, and hit behind the Ute's good leg, bringing the brave to his knees. The knife he had taken from the other warrior he had killed whipped around in a circle and brought forth a gory fountain of blood from a cut throat.

Slocum got to his feet and stood behind the Indian, waiting to make a second thrust. It wasn't necessary. Gurgling and struggling, the Indian collapsed to the ground.

Panting harshly, Slocum retrieved his Colt Navy and looked around to see if he had attracted any attention with the brief, but bloody, fight with the braves.

"Damnation," he said under his breath. Two braves had appeared as if by magic. Both were near their herd of horses. "Where are the rest of you sons of bitches?" He didn't want to fight through the entire Ute nation to get back to Cheyenne.

It looked as if he might have to, though.

The two guarding the horses both carried rifles. Slocum edged around, gauging his chances. He had to get closer before he could use his pistol. They had range and accuracy on him, but he still had a small element of surprise.

One Ute called out. When he got no response, he called again. Slocum wondered if he was calling to the brave who had tried to stick his war lance through him, or some other sentry. When there was no response, the Ute barked something in his lingo to his comrade, and they both started for the edge of the trees.

This suited Slocum just fine. He drew his six-gun and waited until one came within ten feet. Spinning into view, he fired twice. The first bullet caught the brave in the chest. The second missed, but it wasn't needed.

The other brave whirled and fired. The bullet tore past Slocum's head and sent a shower of pinesap raining down on him. Slocum didn't give the Ute a chance for a second shot. He fired fast and accurate, and three bullets ripped through the brave's chest.

The Ute dropped his rifle but refused to die, even with so much lead in him. Turning, he fought to get back into his camp. Slocum rushed after him and dispatched him with the knife. He stepped back and looked at the bloody blade. Three men had died on the knife in the past hour.

Slocum tossed the knife aside. Any more dying by its shining length would be unlucky.

The Utes traveled light, reinforcing his guess that they were a war party on the run from the cavalry. Slocum rummaged through their belongings, looking for anything that might be useful. He found nothing but the rifles dropped by the two warriors guarding the horses. Slocum took one of the rifles and tried to get cartridges from the other, only to find that they were the wrong caliber. Like so many Indians, they carried a hodgepodge of weapons. Most were ancient and sometimes blew up in their faces, but they were better than no rifles at all.

The horses reared and neighed loudly when Slocum approached them, but he singled out the strongest looking pony in the string and concentrated on gentling it. It took several minutes, but Slocum succeeded in mounting. It had been a spell since he'd ridden bareback, but any horse under him was better than none.

"Heeyaw!" he shouted, scattering the other horses. Let the Utes waste time chasing them down. For that matter, let the cavalry pursuing them catch the whole murdering lot. Slocum wasn't feeling too charitable at the moment. He had almost lost his scalp a half dozen times and all because he wanted his brother's watch back.

"Bronston, you've got a load to pay for," Slocum vowed. He used his knees to guide the pony in the direction of Bronston's camp. Going this way meant added danger from the Indians, but he was past caring. He was fuming mad and wouldn't stop until he got his watch back.

Good sense claimed him before he had ridden into the teeth of the Ute war party. He slowed and let his pony find its way north in a giant looping arc. There was some activity in the direction of Bronston's camp, but it didn't sound like a pitched battle. In a way, Slocum hoped the Indians would finish off the major and his men. In another way, he wanted Bronston for himself. Slocum touched the oozing wound on his left arm and remembered what had gotten him into this pickle.

"I want you, Bronston. More'n anybody else, I want you." Slocum gritted his teeth against the pain in his arm and continued his wide path around the camp, finally coming to it from the direction opposite where he had left his two horses.

Dismounting, Slocum neared the camp alert for a trap. He saw no trace of the Utes. Even more curious, he didn't see any of Bronston's men. It was as if they had simply vanished from the face of the earth. He studied the rocky cliff face where the major had posted his lookouts.

Nobody stood guard.

Slocum levered a round into the rifle's chamber and started into Bronston's camp. He had pussyfooted around enough.

"Damnation," he said, looking around. The fire had been kicked to ashes by horses' hooves. All the equipment was gone, as were the men. Slocum couldn't even find the bodies of the men likely to have been killed.

He dropped to one knee and tried to read the signs in the dirt, but there were too many and they were too jumbled for an easy interpretation. The Utes had roared through the camp, of that he was sure from moccasin prints. But what had happened? Two rifle cartridges showed where Bronston's men had tried to defend themselves.

Were they dead? Had Bronston returned and escaped with the survivors? Slocum couldn't tell.

He mounted the Indian pony and trotted down the canyon to where he had left his two horses. They were gone. Cursing, Slocum decided his luck had turned bad again. If he tried to find out what had happened to Bronston, he might end up with a war lance shoved through his back. Only quick reflexes had saved him from this fate earlier.

He wasn't feeling anywhere near as quick or lucky now. His horses were stolen or run off, he had lost Bronston, and the Utes were going to be out for blood when they found the carnage he had left behind in their camp.

The only ray of brightness that Slocum saw was the strong pony under him. At least he didn't have to walk back to Cheyenne. He turned the horse's face down the canyon and urged it forward at as fast a pace as it could comfortably maintain.

15

Slocum almost fell off the Ute pony, then he came awake with a jerk, unaware that he had been nodding off. His arm hurt like fire, and the Wyoming territory around him wavered, as if he was seeing it through a desert's heat mirage in spite of the rugged mountains everywhere. The ride had taken its toll, both in finding Bronston and everything that had happened afterward.

He had spent only a few hours trying to find Bronston. Returning to Cheyenne on one unsaddled pony took a full day. He blinked and shook himself to be sure he wasn't hallucinating. The dusty streets of the small town were stretched out in front of him. Slocum gripped the pony's bridle and steered it toward civilization, hoping he hadn't drifted into a fever dream. Then he knew he had returned. The pony shied, not liking the smells coming from the town.

To Slocum they were more heavenly than anything he'd ever found before.

As he rode through town, he knew people were watching him. He tried to sit straighter on the horse but only sagged.

"Hey, mister, you all right?" someone called.

"Fine, just fine. Thanks for asking," Slocum called back. That was the last thing he remembered before falling off the horse.

He heard frightened neighing, the clatter of hooves, and the sounds of people whispering. Then blackness closed entirely around him, wrapping him in a warm, soft shroud.

"You sew a finer stitch than I ever could," Slocum heard a distant voice saying. "My wife's tried to teach me, but it's no use."

"This is the first time I've ever used my skills on a person," came a voice Slocum fought to recognize. It was soft and feminine and he knew it. He knew it, but recognition kept slipping away. He succumbed to the gentle flow of dark tides washing over him again.

When he came to a second time, he sat bolt upright in bed.

"I do declare, John, you simply cannot relax, can you?" Ruth Waddell sat in a straight-backed chair beside his bed. "You've run a high fever from your wound, the doctor said."

"Doctor?" Slocum said, trying to piece everything together. He held up his left arm and saw clean white bandages over the cut Bronston had given him.

"The doctor," Ruth said firmly. "I happened to see you being carried into his office. That was a nasty cut."

"You sewed it up," Slocum said, remembering the snippets he had heard before. How long before? Days?

"Yes. You may thank me later. It was quite a grisly task, I must say. I have never done anything quite so . . . messy before."

"How long have I slept?"

"Unconscious is more like it," Ruth said, putting away a small basket containing sewing. "You've been here two days."

Slocum groaned. He had ridden a full day getting back to Cheyenne—at least he remembered one. And now he had been in bed for another two. Bronston had another three-day head start on them.

"We've got to get on the trail. Your father's. . . ."

"Don't fret over him, John. While you've been out getting yourself all sliced to bloody strips, I have been asking after him. What I've learned will aid us in finding him quickly."

"From that old galoot? The one whose mind wandered?" Slocum lay back and tried to put his thoughts into order. Ruth said he'd been down with fever. That explained the odd images still fluttering through his head.

He flexed his left hand, and the fingers felt weak. It would take a few days of use before he regained his usual power in that hand. Holding his horse's reins would do it. But his gun hand was all right, that was all he needed to hold his Colt and put a few rounds through Bronston's worthless hide.

"He led me to another citizen, a prospector whom Father questioned at some length. I have a map that will direct us to a scenic spot where Father must surely have lingered to take photographs."

Ruth looked at him, then asked, "Are you feeling any better? You are so pale."

"The fever," Slocum said. "It's eaten away at me."

"What happened out there?" the brunette asked, moving her chair closer. "You must have fought incredible battles. Did you find Major Bronston?"

"I had him. I *had* him, and he got away," Slocum lamented, the memories replaying to torment him further. "I'll never get my watch back because Bronston was—" Slocum cut off his explanation when he heard the door open. A man and two Army officers entered. The man carried a stethoscope in his hand.

"Keep on with your explanation of what went on, Mr. Slocum," urged the doctor. "These two gents are real interested in hearing how you came by a Ute pony."

The taller of the uniformed pair, a captain, said, "We've been chasing a party of more than twenty Utes for almost a month. They keep a jump ahead of us."

"How the hell did you end up with one of their mounts?" demanded the other officer, a blond lieutenant who probably did not have to shave more than once a week.

Slocum ignored the lieutenant and addressed his question to the captain. "Where did they come from? There's no Ute reservation around here."

"They're from southwestern Colorado. The leader is Banded Snake and he's taken it into his head to kill every cavalry trooper he can find."

Slocum nodded, remembering how the war party had gone after Bronston when they saw his Union officer's jacket.

"How did you get one of their horses?" the lieutenant asked, his voice almost breaking.

"I took it," Slocum said. "I walked into their camp, killed five of their braves, chose which horse I wanted from their string, and rode on back to Cheyenne."

The lieutenant took a step forward, as if to strike Slocum. The doctor stepped between them, blocking the angry officer.

"This man's been through a great deal, Lieutenant Moss. The fever might have left him a bit touched in the head. You understand?" The doctor spoke as if to the room, but stared at the captain.

The senior officer took his lieutenant aside and sent him on some errand, then turned his attention back to Slocum.

"Any information you can give, Mr. Slocum, would be greatly appreciated." The captain stared hard at him, as if trying to figure out the truth of what Slocum had just told them about stealing the pony. He came to some sort of decision because he said, "I apologize for the lieutenant's behavior. We've been on the trail for well nigh a month and we're all getting a mite testy."

"Ten or twelve hours ride north of here is where I came across their camp. I scattered their horses when I stole the one I rode back on."

"What possessed you to steal a horse from Banded Snake?" The captain's question was an honest one.

"I lost mine," Slocum said simply. He started to ask about Bronston, but held back. Slocum had no love for Union officers, even though he didn't have anything personal against this one.

"You get sliced up like that and still can steal a Ute pony." The captain cocked his head and added, "And you killed five of Banded Snake's braves."

"Reckon so," Slocum said.

"You're one tough hombre. I don't want to cross you again." The captain settled his wide-brimmed hat on his head, about-faced, and marched from the room.

"Never seen Cap'n Jack so curt before," the doctor said. "He must have thought you were lying to him."

"Or that I wasn't," Slocum said, suddenly very tired. "Can I get some sleep?" He yawned and lay back on the bed. He heard Ruth say something he didn't quite catch, then he was sound asleep.

"Two more days," Slocum complained. "We're almost a week behind now."

"John, you required the time to heal," Ruth Waddell said. "I prepared for the trip. Using some of the money you left,

I bought more supplies. They ought to be adequate to last for several weeks, or so the store keeper assured me."

Slocum groaned when he saw the mountain of goods the merchant had sold her. Even here there wasn't any such thing as an honest businessman. The salt pork was growing blue fur, and the cans were battered, some of them were ready to explode from the gases inside. Slocum had opened enough like them in his day to know the least he'd get was a bellyache if he ate the contents. He had seen strong men die within eight hours after eating goods from a bulging can.

"We need to travel lighter," he said. He went through the pile, and separated out the useful from the decaying. When he finished, Slocum had to sit and rest. The fever from his wound still wore him down.

"Let me see your arm. The doctor said to change the dressing every few hours."

"That won't be necessary," he said, but Slocum didn't protest too much when Ruth sat beside him and began unwrapping the linen. He saw the precise stitches that marched up his arm, closing the gaping wound Bronston had given him. Ruth had done a good enough job that there might not even be a noticeable scar when it healed.

"There," she said, as she finished dabbing it with a solution that burned like fire. "The doctor says he doesn't often see men who heal as fast as you. You're very lucky, John." She turned her brown eyes up and stared into his green ones. "But you never have told me how you came by this terrible wound."

"The others ended up worse," Slocum said, not wanting to get into yarn spinning. He owed Bronston for more than stealing his watch. Slocum didn't know when their trails would cross again, but when it happened, Slocum was going to be ready. This time he'd shoot the son of a bitch straight out and worry about getting answers later.

"That's no answer," she said, heaving a deep sigh. "You can be a most vexing man."

"I want to get on the trail as soon as possible," Slocum said. He wished he still had the Ute pony, but when he had fallen off it, the horse had bolted and run from town. Someone might have lassoed it, but they were keeping that fact to themselves. It had been a valiant animal and had served him well.

"You encountered the Indians Captain Tyler asked about," Ruth said. "Everyone says you were riding a captured Ute horse when you rode into Cheyenne. But what of Major Bronston? Did you find him? Did something happen that makes you so closed mouth?"

"He's on the trail ahead of us by at least a week. He's got one or two fewer men riding with him than he had before I found him," Slocum said, figuring the one named Joe was dead and maybe his partner from up on the mountainside, as well. He didn't know about Dickensen or the other man who had been at the campfire. Slocum reckoned they faced three or four left in that party.

And more than fifteen Utes out for blood.

"Will you ever tell me what you found, John?"

"Get the horses. There's still a goodly six hours of daylight left. We can be ten miles out of Cheyenne by nightfall."

He wished for the bright moonlight he had ridden out under a week earlier, but it was long gone. Riding with Ruth would slow his pace, also. She would never be able to keep up any kind of speed after the sun went down.

"Very well," she said, angry with him. She flounced off. Slocum watched her go and wondered at the old saw about an angry woman being a beautiful one. In Ruth Waddell's case, it was certainly so, but right now his mind was more on revenge than love.

They rode down Cheyenne's main street and headed north. The only person watching them leave was the undertaker. The short, stout man had a baleful expression on his face. Slocum snorted and urged his horse along faster. The mortician obviously felt cheated out of a client.

Slocum vowed to keep cheating the undertakers as long as possible—and to deliver Bronston to them.

They rode in silence for almost an hour before Ruth's natural enthusiasm bubbled over past her anger.

"I can't wait to see what photographs he's taken," she said suddenly. "Father's trip has been remarkable. The scenery has been superb, and with his skill as a photographer, it will look even better once printed properly."

"A picture can never match the real thing," Slocum said, his mind a hundred miles off. Devils Tower was a week's travel north. Getting there they'd have to cross a half dozen big rivers, the Platte being the worst of the lot, and find their way through mountainous country. It might be quicker to head north and west, find the central valley running down Wyoming's middle from Antelope Springs, then cut back toward Devils Tower when they reached the Powder River.

"Perhaps it's not the same as seeing it firsthand, but most of the people who would buy Father's picture book will never get the chance to see the West for themselves."

"You're saying it's a safe way to see all this?" Slocum waved his arm to indicate the soaring mountains covered with pine forests and the rest of the blue haze-cloaked distance.

"That is true." She looked at him in amazement. "You disapprove, don't you? You don't want Father coming out here and recording his photographs. Why not?"

"Besides the trouble it's already caused," Slocum said, "he might be too good."

"I don't understand."

"Folks back East will look at the photographs and want to come out here for themselves. I don't want the land filling up. I reckon I like it just as it is."

Ruth started to laugh, then bit it off when she saw he was serious. "You are a strange man, John Slocum."

"Been called worse. About time to trade horses."

They made good time going north using the map Ruth had made from the prospector's recollection. To his surprise, Slocum followed the crude drawing with no trouble. He angled up between Fort Laramie and Hartville, getting across the Platte easier than they had any right. The landmarks were precisely noted, and Slocum began to hope that they'd come across Phillip Waddell in a few days.

"How long does your father spend at any given place taking his photographs?" Slocum asked, as much to pass the time as to keep Ruth happy.

"That depends on the quality of the light and the other elements that go into taking a good picture. Wyoming seems comprised of excellent photographic qualities. It will make his book a real sensation. I am sure of it."

Slocum didn't say anything about Ruth's enthusiasm for the land. Nor did he remind her she was seeking out her father to tell him of his wife's death. He knew the risks they took following the elusive photographer but Ruth didn't.

Bronston was a problem, but Slocum thought the renegade Utes were more of a problem. Even with the cavalry troop hunting for them, the Indians could cause more mischief than a handful of former Union soldiers.

Thinking about the Utes, Slocum slowed the pace and studied the ground before the sun dipped too low in the west. At just about Chugwater Creek, Slocum saw that the trail was cut up, but it was mostly from shod hooves, and the prints were old. He didn't see any sign of the cavalry troop, but he hadn't expected to. He and Ruth had decided to ride north and a bit to the east and Slocum had steered the cavalry captain to the north and west, on the other side of a decent-sized ridge.

"You are worried about them finding us, aren't you?" asked Ruth. "Did the Indians cut you up? I heard horrible stories of torture while waiting for you back in Cheyenne. I was so worried."

"The Utes didn't cut me up," Slocum said. "Fact is, they only gave me a few scratches."

"Then you were joking about killing five of them." Ruth let out a sigh of relief, as if concerned for his mortal soul. "No one really believed you when you told the captain that story."

"Fever does strange things to a man's mind," Slocum said obliquely. The sun had gone down far enough to make him hunt for a campsite. He found a tumble of rocks and a sandy spit that looked inviting. Kicking his heels into his horse's flanks, he led his spare mount and the pack mule into the secluded area.

"A good place," Ruth said, looking up at the towering boulders around the sandy area. "No one will be able to see a fire from the trail." She looked at him sharply and asked, "That was why you chose this location?"

"I've been through too much this past week. Let's just say I don't cotton much to having unexpected visitors dropping in on us."

Slocum scouted the area and found a sentry point high in the rocks. While Ruth prepared the fire and fixed a simple dinner, he sat and stared at the trail stretching back toward Cheyenne. Slocum worried that they hadn't come far enough fast enough. One thing was in their favor— no one tracked them. He would have spotted any sign of pursuit, from Indians, or Bronston, or even the cavalry.

Slocum didn't like the threat Captain Tyler had made, it seemed as if he might stop by the sheriff's office and thumb through his stack of wanted posters. The Utes were the officer's primary concern, but an outlaw captured along the way—especially one wanted for judge killing—would go a long way toward soothing any ruffled feathers over the failure to stop Banded Snake.

"John, supper is ready. Come down and eat. You're looking a mite peaked from the day's ride."

Slocum slid down the rough boulder and landed in a crouch in the sand. He put his new rifle against the rock and sat down beside Ruth near the fire. Without a word he took the tin plate she offered and ate, not really tasting the food. His mind drifted to all that had happened.

"You're dwelling on bad things, John," Ruth said, taking the plate from him. He looked around, startled.

"What?"

"You are thinking of all the evil things that happened while you were gone, which you will not tell me about." Ruth moved closer. Her hand reached out and touched his rough chin, then stroked across his cheek.

"I'm not keeping anything important from you," Slocum protested.

"Hush. Let me give you some of my special medicine. You look to be strong enough for it now."

She kissed him full on the lips. It took Slocum a second to respond. Ruth was right. He was worrying about things that were over and done. He had to look to the future. To the present. To Ruth Waddell.

The brunette gently pushed him back onto their blankets. With the fire at their feet, she snuggled closer to him. Slocum felt her lush body pressing into his and knew what he had been missing this past week. Reaching out, he cupped her firm breasts and squeezed gently. She sighed in contentment.

Through the fabric of her blouse he felt her nipples beginning to harden. His left hand was still a bit clumsy but he managed to unfasten the buttons marching down the front of Ruth's blouse and lift the frilly undergarment he found. The woman's white breasts gleamed in the flickering light from the fire.

Slocum bent over and took one hard nubbin into his mouth, sucking greedily. The woman arched her back and tried to push the entire marshmallowy mound into his mouth.

"You make me feel so good, John. So good, so good!"

His hands began roaming with more confidence. He lifted her skirt and found an inner thigh that now danced with muscle from all the riding she had done in the past weeks. He stroked up and down, every time moving just a bit farther up.

When he found the furry triangle nestled between the woman's thighs, a ripple of desire passed through her body. She clung to him fiercely and whispered in his ear, "Take me now. Don't wait. I need you so. I've *needed* you since you left."

Together they got Slocum's jeans unfastened. He wiggled free and rolled on top of Ruth. She eagerly kissed, stroked, and urged him on. Her knees came up on either side of his body as he moved into position. His hardened length touched her nether lips, gently brushing across them.

Electric shocks passed through both of them. Slocum knew he couldn't tease and torment her any longer. He moved up, found his target, and then plunged in with ferocious need. Ruth returned his desire. She locked her ankles behind his back and pulled him even deeper into her yearning interior.

Slocum lost track of time. He moved and Ruth responded. He felt her all around him crushing down pleasurably, and giving him as much as he gave her. Then his hips took complete control and moved on their own. Slocum rocked back and forth, trying to split the woman in half.

Ruth gasped and arched her back, while grinding her crotch into his. He saw the red flush rising from the tops of her breasts to her shoulders and neck, and knew there was nothing to worry about. He relaxed just enough to allow the white-hot rush from his loins to spew forth.

Spent, Slocum sank forward. Ruth's arms circled him and held him close. They kissed a while longer, then sleep crept up on Slocum and took him away. His last conscious thought was that there might never be a time again like this moment.

16

Slocum awoke just before dawn with an uneasy feeling gnawing at him. He stretched and dislodged Ruth from her position next to him. She stirred, muttered something in her sleep that he couldn't make out, and then rolled over, pulling the blanket around her shoulders. Slocum pushed himself to a sitting position and felt the cold wind blowing off the high mountains. He appreciated the coolness in the face of a hot summer down on the plains. He would take the high country to Kansas anytime in the summer, and maybe even in the winter. He didn't see that the winters were any less intense at higher elevations than they were on the plains. He had ridden out too many blue northers whipping down from Canada and watched as they froze livestock and humans throughout Iowa, Nebraska, and Kansas to cotton much to that country.

He dressed quickly and tried to figure out what was making him so edgy. Going to the horses, he stopped and listened. They were also skittish, but that meant nothing. A coyote or wolf may have spooked them. Taking his rifle, Slocum climbed the rocks surrounding their camp and found a good observation point.

For several minutes he saw nothing unusual, but he had learned that patience was as important a trait as any, and it could keep him alive when others rushed about blindly. The first rays of dawn had yet to lighten the sky, but he saw strange flickerings in the distance. Squinting and trying to get as good a look as possible, Slocum realized this couldn't be light from a false dawn—not unless the sun had taken to rising in the north.

"Campfires," he muttered. "And lots of them." He made out three distinct fires, then a fourth. Someone was up and about early, but who might it be? Slocum considered the time between the cavalry captain's interrogation and the distance to the north, and doubted the fires belonged to his troopers.

Bronston? Why would he have so many fires? One would do for his small group.

"Utes," he decided. Slocum slumped a little. To detour now would add days or even a week to their travel. He felt time pressing down heavily on his shoulders, knowing that Bronston and Dickensen were at least a week ahead. The former major and his aide might not know the precise location where Phillip Waddell had gone to shoot his photographs, but a week was a considerable amount of time to spend looking for someone, even in a place as vast as Wyoming.

"What is it, John?" came Ruth Waddell's soft voice. Slocum spun around and almost fell from his perch on the rock. He had been so intent on studying the campfires that he hadn't heard her approaching.

"We'll either have to go around the Utes or wait a day or two and let them move on," he said. "There's no way I'm going to tangle with fifteen or more Ute warriors who are madder'n a wet hen at me right now." Slocum wasn't sure they would recognize him as the one who had killed five of their party, but he doubted Banded Snake really much cared who he killed right now.

The Indians were on a tear, and killing was their only way of getting back at the white man for all the injustice heaped upon them.

"There might be another way, John," Ruth pointed out. "That cavalry captain is hunting for them, isn't he? Why don't we find where he has gone and steer him in the right direction?"

"They left town and headed north. They should have found the Utes." He stared at the campfires, now slowly vanishing as daylight marched across the land. In a few minutes it would take a spyglass to see the small columns of smoke from the fires. And then they would vanish entirely as the air heated and began to shimmer a mite.

"Look around. Maybe you'll see them."

Slocum wondered if the campfires might not belong to the troopers. The military was fond of rising before dawn and tormenting its men. He had only guessed as to the nature of the men sitting around the fires and eating their breakfasts.

"There, John, see over there?" Ruth stood and pointed off to the northeast. "I think those might be campfires, too. My eyes aren't quite as sharp as yours, but they look right."

Slocum turned in the direction Ruth pointed. He nodded slowly. There was another camp, maybe as many as fifty men from the size of those fires. The ones he had spotted before were gone in the morning light. These continued to be visible for long minutes, showing how much larger they were.

"Why would the cavalry troop advertise its position like that?" he asked, more to himself than to Ruth. It didn't make any sense for the cavalry captain to allow his men to build such huge fires if they might be spotted by the Utes. The cavalry's stated mission was to round up the Indians, not drive them off—or present themselves as obvious ambush candidates.

"That lieutenant wasn't too knowledgeable, was he?" asked Ruth.

Slocum had to admit she was right. Left to his own devices, the shavetail lieutenant might do any number of things wrong, even to the point of courting disaster. Slocum marked him as a man who would never accept friendly advice because he thought he knew it all. And woe to any experienced sergeant who hinted broadly that there might be a better way of setting up a bivouac.

"The cavalry can't be more than a dozen miles off. We could reach them before noon, if we rode fast," Slocum said. "*If* that's a cavalry detachment. It might be the Utes. And *that* might be the cavalry," he said indicating the spot where he had seen the four campfires.

"We can sit and wait for them to both clear out," Ruth said. "We know where Father is most likely taking his photographs. There's not that much of a rush, is there?"

Slocum didn't answer. He had the feeling in his gut that there was. Bronston wasn't the kind of man who dawdled. Whatever grudge he had against Phillip Waddell he wanted settled fast. And Slocum kept coming back to the simple fact that he wanted a piece of Bronston's hide for his own. The man had stolen his watch, tried to kill him, and generally deserved to be left as buzzard food.

"Break camp," Slocum said as he came to a decision. "We ride for those campfires." He pointed to the northwest. Slocum didn't want to go into his reasoning about Bronston and Dickensen with Ruth. She was eager to see her father again, and Slocum didn't want to arrive just as Bronston finished butchering Phillip Waddell.

• • •

They rode hard all morning switching horses every forty-five minutes instead of every hour. Even so, they were still tired, and the horses were approaching the point of exhaustion when they came upon Captain Tyler and a squad of men beside the trail, eating their noonday meal.

"Slocum, what are you doing here?" Tyler demanded.

"You want those Utes?" Slocum said, not bothering to bandy words. "I saw their fires just before dawn, not fifteen miles due east of here. If you fan out and ride hard, you can snare the lot of them before they know what's happening."

"Really?" The captain looked skeptical. "How'd you happen to find us?"

"I saw your bonfires. Damned stupid thing to do, building fires that big when you're chasing down an enemy as wily as Banded Snake," Slocum said. From the way Tyler's eyebrows rose he knew Ruth had been right. The fires were Lieutenant Moss's doing, and the captain knew nothing of them.

"Bonfires, is it?" Captain Tyler scratched his chin and shook his head. "Where is the Ute war party?"

"I can help you scout them out, if you like. I've had some experience."

"Why don't you and George Fourkiller head that way and reconnoiter?" The captain pointed to an Indian in buckskins sitting alone by the side of the road.

"Pawnee?" Slocum asked.

"Cherokee. Damned fine tracker, but we haven't found a trace of Banded Snake's party so far."

Slocum turned to Ruth and said, "You stay with the captain. We should be back before nightfall."

"But what will we do then?" asked Ruth. From Slocum's expression she knew the answer. All she said was, "Oh."

Slocum and George Fourkiller had a lot of riding to do, and then the troopers would probably have some fighting ahead of them.

"They couldn't have gone far from where I saw them camped this morning," Slocum said to the dour Cherokee. Fourkiller nodded and studied the ground, running his fingers over the shallow impressions in the dirt.

"I make it at least fifteen," Slocum said, knowing already how many warriors remained in the Ute war party. George Fourkiller looked up and nodded in agreement, then turned back to his work.

Slocum was anxious to return to the cavalry company and get the troopers into the fray. Bronston was a week ahead, and he could not let the major reach Phillip Waddell before his daughter found him.

"We go," the Cherokee said, startling Slocum. These were the first words George Fourkiller had spoken in more than three hours.

"What do you think?"

"We can trap them there." The Cherokee pointed to the north, through a narrow pass. "They are on this side now. They will go through there soon. We wait. We kill."

How the tracker got all this from the spoor was beyond Slocum. He had seen men better at tracking than he was, and most of them were Indians, but never had he come across one who could be this specific from such small clues.

"You want to stay here and let me go back or do you—" Slocum bit off his words when Fourkiller held up his hand and pointed to his ear.

At first Slocum heard nothing. Then faint echoes of hooves came to him.

"Banded Snake," the Cherokee said. "Close. We both

must return." Fourkiller vaulted into the saddle and turned his horse's face toward the east. He never bothered to see if Slocum was following. There wasn't any reason for Slocum to stay and fight the Utes by himself. They had taken three hours coming out. It took less than two before they came across the cavalry company.

"Captain!" Slocum called, waving his hat. Tyler had rejoined the main body of his troop and had gotten them moving in the right direction. Slocum had hopes of George Fourkiller's plan being put into effect before sundown. He wanted to see the Utes removed, if for no other reason than to clear the countryside of a potential impediment to finding Phillip Waddell.

"Wait a few minutes, Slocum. Let me talk with my scout." The captain and George Fourkiller talked with some animation for several minutes. From the broad grin on Tyler's face, Slocum knew he approved of the Cherokee scout's plan. He didn't bother checking with Slocum. He issued immediate orders for the company to wheel right and start for the narrow pass.

Slocum rode back and joined Ruth. To his surprise Lieutenant Moss was with her.

"John, you're back. I'm so glad," she said, casting a sidelong glance at the junior officer. "Lieutenant Moss was assigned to watch over me while we traveled."

Slocum almost burst out laughing. The lieutenant's sour expression told how desirable an assignment this was for him. He had made a huge blunder in allowing the bonfires to be built when the troop should have been lying low, and now he was paying the price for it. In the young officer's mind, guarding Ruth would be one step shy of a general court-martial for cowardice.

Slocum thought the young officer would find more than enough action before the day was out.

Captain Tyler rode along the column, speaking with his non-coms and getting them ready for what might be a vicious fight. He finally turned his horse and rode beside Slocum and Ruth.

"We're going to hit them just about where you suggested, Slocum," the captain said, as if the words burned his tongue. "George thinks highly of your skills."

"It's the other way around," Slocum said. "I learned how to really track from him. I swear, he could track a honeybee in a snowstorm."

"By smell alone," Captain Tyler agreed. He turned in the saddle and pointed in the direction of the narrow pass Slocum had noticed. "There's where we take them. I'm having Moss take a squad and set up a cross fire. The remainder of the company will drive the Utes forward."

"Sweep around and try to snare them in a net?" Slocum frowned. He preferred an outright ambush. This tactic posed real problems. If Banded Snake decided to make a stand, no section of Tyler's line would be strong enough to hold, and the Utes would escape.

"I know what you're thinking, Slocum. It's a chance I'm willing to take. You and the lady don't have to take part." The way Captain Tyler spoke made it clear he wanted no civilians nearby to worry over. Slocum cast a sidelong glance at Lieutenant Moss. The young man's face positively glowed at the notion that he was going to be allowed a real soldier's role instead of wet-nursing a civilian woman.

"That's fine with us," Slocum said, still worrying about how tight the captain's sweeping line of cavalry was likely to be. The foothills had too many ravines and cutbacks that would allow a clever adversary the chance to get away. And hiding in the forested areas would make rooting out the Indians even more difficult if they decided to stand their ground and fight, rather than run.

The only way the cavalry captain was going to come out looking like a hero was if Banded Snake spooked, and tried to flee without scouting ahead to see what he was running into.

"Thank you for your help. I must say I misjudged you," Captain Tyler said. He shouted over his shoulder, "Lieutenant Moss, to the front of the column!" Tyler galloped off leaving Slocum and Ruth behind. Slocum slowed their progress and let the column pass. He watched their dust and worried even more. There wasn't much way that this many men could spring a trap unless their prey was deaf, dumb, and blind.

Banded Snake was none of those.

"What's wrong, John?"

"They're riding into deep trouble," he said. "The Utes aren't going to roll over and play dead like some hound dog."

"That's their problem now, isn't it? We have to get back on Father's trail." Ruth fumbled out the map she had of the meadow to the south of Devils Tower, where her father was supposed to be shooting his photographs. Slocum paid her scant attention.

"This trouble is closer at hand," he told her. "If the Utes aren't nabbed the way Tyler wants, they'll scatter across the countryside and some of them will be going in our direction. The only thing worse than a Ute war party is a lone warrior whose war party has just been slaughtered."

"You're saying they won't be happy?"

"They'll be angrier than a scalded dog," Slocum said. He tried to figure where the safest spot for them would be. No matter where he looked, he found trouble.

"We can simply go to ground for a day and. . . ." Ruth understood what she was saying and bit off the rest of the sentence. "I see the problem. We would be no better off sitting out the Indians' escape than we would be letting them ride past. We lose time either way."

"The only way we don't is if we can get through the pass Captain Tyler is trying to close off." Slocum estimated times and how difficult the travel would be, and shook his head. There wasn't any chance of getting through the pass before the shavetail Moss took his snipers into the throat of the pass.

"Oh, look, John, there's the captain's scout. He is coming back."

Slocum watched as the Cherokee scout rode up to them. George Fourkiller reined back and simply stared for several minutes. Ruth got uneasy and started to speak, but Slocum motioned her to silence. If the scout wanted to talk, it was up to him to start. Fourkiller might come to his own decision and simply ride off, and if he did, that would be fine with Slocum, too.

"He's wrong," George Fourkiller finally said. "Can you talk to him?"

"To Captain Tyler?" Slocum shook his head. "He's got it into his head that Banded Snake will turn tail and run."

"Won't matter if he does," the Cherokee scout said. He spat to show what he thought of Tyler's ability.

"You got any ideas?" Slocum curled his leg around his pommel and waited as Fourkiller worked through what bothered him most.

"We can help. You. Me. Up in the pass."

"I've some skill with a rifle," Slocum allowed, "but two rifles won't matter that much if Banded Snake tries to break through to the other side of the pass."

"Might." George Fourkiller reached into his saddlebags and pulled out five sticks of dynamite.

Slocum wanted to laugh. The Cherokee came prepared for any size war. Slocum said, "Why not let the captain use that? Or Moss? He'll do most anything to keep from looking like a horse's rear end."

George Fourkiller spat again and put the dynamite back into his saddlebags. He said nothing. Slocum had to make up his own mind about what to do.

"John, he's suggesting you and he go into the pass and single-handedly take on the Utes, isn't he?"

"Seems that way," Slocum said. "This is one way to be sure we get through the pass." He turned over all the possible obstacles they might encounter in his head, and realized he was risking his neck when all he had to lose was a day or two of travel.

Slocum stiffened and slid his leg away from the pommel. The memory of David James Bronston burned in his head and heart. Even one day separating them might be bad for Phillip Waddell—and Slocum's chances of getting his revenge on the renegade major.

"We'll find a safe spot for you, Ruth," he said, coming to a decision. "This will work better for us, Fourkiller and me doing Moss's work for him."

"John, no." Ruth Waddell started to protest the danger, then saw the set of his jaw. She subsided, realizing Slocum was going to be caught up in the middle of the fight, no matter what she said or did. The brunette took a deep breath and said, "Where do you want me to wait?"

Slocum and George Fourkiller had been on foot for more than an hour. They listened to Lieutenant Moss's men blundering around, trying to find good sniper positions along the rocky walls of the narrow pass. The lieutenant barked orders, mostly contradictory, and created even more confusion among his squad.

"He'll learn," Slocum told the Cherokee scout. He remembered his own days during the war. He had been promoted up through the ranks, but the jump between sergeant and lieutenant had been a big one for a young man. Slocum had let it go to his head—until he got a patrol killed because of his bullheaded orders. By the time he made the rank of captain, he had learned a great deal.

"So many will die," the scout said sadly. "Some are good men. Others, eh." He made a slashing motion with his hand showing he didn't much care what became of those men.

Slocum studied the pass and found the proper spots to place the dynamite. They didn't need more than the four sticks to create a diversion. If they brought down a few big boulders, they could break any concerted rush to escape through the pass. If the Utes were thrown into disarray for even a few minutes, Moss's snipers would cut them down with little chance of reprisal.

"Good work," George Fourkiller said. The Cherokee looked up into the sky, then put his back to a rock and tipped his flat-brimmed hat down. Slocum heard loud snores within a minute.

He wasn't as comfortable with their preparations as the Cherokee. Slocum checked his rifle, just in case it was needed. He studied the pass and found stony pockets where Utes might take refuge, and mentally reassigned the snipers to take those into account. He wasn't completely satisfied with Moss's deployment, but it wasn't as bad as it could have been.

Finally realizing he was driving himself crazy, Slocum dropped down beside the Cherokee scout and pulled his Stetson over his eyes. It would be dark in another couple hours. Captain Tyler had to make his sweep and chase Banded Snake into the pass before then, or the wily Indian would be able to slip through.

Slocum came awake with a start when he heard gunfire. He grabbed his Winchester and got to his feet. George

Fourkiller was already in position, sighting along his old Henry's barrel at the first stick of dynamite. Slocum sat beside him resting the rifle on a rock and aiming it at the second stick of dynamite. They had cut themselves a hard shot on each of the four sticks, but Slocum was up to it. He knew men and their abilities and saw that Fourkiller had the confidence to make his shots.

"There," Slocum said. In the mouth of the pass rose a cloud of dust. Captain Tyler's sweep was working, as much as Slocum had doubted that it would.

"Let us fire now," the Cherokee said. "We—"

"Damn him!" shouted Slocum when he saw what was happening. Moss wasn't content with letting his men stay under cover and shoot the Ute warriors as they were jammed into the pass by the remainder of his company.

"He makes a frontal attack," George Fourkiller said in amazement. Slocum hadn't thought anything would amaze the scout, but then he had never seen anything this stupid this side of Pickett's Charge.

Moss had exposed his men and was having them rush down into the narrow floor of the pass to engage the Ute in what could only be a slaughter for the unmounted cavalry soldiers.

17

"Fire!" Slocum shouted to George Fourkiller. "Set off the charges! Now!"

The only way Slocum could see of saving any of Lieutenant Moss's troopers was to use the dynamite. Fourkiller started shooting his revolving Henry and hit a charge with his fifth round. Slocum did better, setting off the dynamite he had sighted in on with only two rounds. The rumble and cascade of falling rock and dust momentarily slowed the frontal assault ordered by Moss.

This might have saved one or two of the men. Slocum wasn't sure it kept any more than that from being cut to bloody ribbons by the approaching Ute war party.

Slocum shot several more times until his magazine fetched up empty. He missed the third charge with every round. He turned and looked down into the rocky notch. A few rounds among the Indians on their ponies would do more good than another small landslide. Slocum slammed the cartridges into his Winchester, then began methodically firing. The confusion masked most of what was happening.

He was sure he winged one Indian. The Ute let out a shrill screech and tumbled off his paint, but mostly Slocum just added to the confusion with his shots. George Fourkiller was doing little better with his old rifle. Several times the Cherokee's revolving cylinder came up empty and he took time to reload.

"They're going to be a lot of graves tonight," Slocum said, chancing a look over the top of the rock where he rested his rifle. "And not many of them are going to be Ute graves."

The Cherokee shrugged as if saying, What do you expect when you put a new lieutenant in charge? Fourkiller swung around again and began firing slowly. Slocum saw that the battle had intensified on the floor of the pass. Moss had gotten most of his men down now, and Banded Snake's warriors had the advantage being on horseback. They were faster and presented targets moving too fast for the troopers to stop.

"They're breaking through," Slocum said angrily. He hadn't liked Captain Tyler's plan, but he had never thought Moss would try pushing the Ute back into the stronger cavalry force with a direct assault. All the lieutenant had to do was sit high up on the rocks and bushwhack the Indians.

"He wanted a medal, glory, others to worship him. Now he dies a fool," George Fourkiller said. Slocum didn't have to ask who the Cherokee was talking about. Moss would be the laughingstock of a hundred cavalry posts. That didn't bother Slocum as much as losing the men who had obeyed such stupid orders.

"Banded Snake's braves are going through Moss's squad like shit through a goose," Slocum said. He got off a few more shots and winged another Ute. He felt like he was dipping water from the Colorado River with a teaspoon. Every single shot looked good until he saw the force building behind his target.

"Tyler will never stop the Utes now," the Cherokee said. Slocum knew it was true. Once Banded Snake rode by

Moss, every shot from Captain Tyler's company would have to go through Moss's position. The troopers would be shooting at their own men.

Slocum turned back to the two dynamite charges remaining on the side of the mountain. It was getting dark in the high-walled pass, and he hadn't been too accurate before. He had not taken the time needed to properly sight in his new rifle, and for that he cursed himself. A few hours work would have made this an easy shot.

Slocum began firing, carefully aiming and watching where the bullet ricocheted off rock. His fifth shot set off another dynamite charge. He turned immediately to the remaining stick of dynamite. Fourkiller saw what he intended and joined in, adding the rounds from his Henry to those of Slocum's Winchester.

Who hit the dynamite Slocum never knew, but it had the proper effect. The ground rumbled as a huge boulder came apart and cracked down the middle. Tiny edges of it began to crumble, and then the entire rock slid down into the pass. Slocum was blinded by the cloud of dust rushing up from the floor of the pass. He ducked down behind a protecting rock and took the chance to reload.

"We have done what we can," George Fourkiller said. "We should retreat."

"And get shot by Moss?" Slocum countered. "He's gone wild down there." Bullets flew through the air, ricocheting in all directions. The only saving grace Slocum could see to such undisciplined firing was that something had to hit the enemy, even if by accident. The rock fall might have slowed Banded Snake, and the fusillade would cut down a few more of his braves. If nothing else, a bullet or two would down the Ute horses.

The thunder from the small avalanche did not diminish. Slocum looked up higher on the cliff faces, worrying he had started a real landslide. The last of the rock had slumped down into the pass. This roar came from some other source.

Captain Tyler led his men in full attack, galloping past Moss's men on the ground and straight into Banded Snake's rear. The Indians milled in confusion from the rock falls, the wild firing, and now Tyler's assault. Slocum didn't know how it had happened but the tide had turned once more. The Utes were surrendering and the cavalry had won.

"Is it always this way?" he asked the Cherokee scout. All he got for an answer was a broad grin.

Slocum and George Fourkiller stayed behind the rock until the last of the shots had died out. Slocum tentatively showed himself, waving his bandanna to keep from being cut down by Moss or one of the unrestrained snipers. Only when Slocum wasn't shot up did Fourkiller stand and hold up his rifle to show he wasn't a threat, either. Together, they made their way down the side of the pass.

Captain Tyler had a tight circle of troopers around Banded Snake and his men. Slocum did a quick count. There had been almost thirty Utes when he first encountered them. Only ten remained, and if he and George Fourkiller hadn't planted the dynamite charges, more might have escaped to the other side of the pass.

Slocum shuddered when he thought about what might have happened then. Tyler would have found their positions reversed. Banded Snake would have had the cavalry penned up in the narrow pass and would have shot the soldiers like fish in a barrel.

"What's in store for them?" Slocum asked.

"We'll escort them back to southwestern Colorado and their reservation. Any punitive action is up to the government agents." Tyler looked around, taking silent roll of his own men. Slocum wasn't sure but the surprise on the captain's face showed more had been lost than any of them had suspected.

"You owe a debt to your scout," Slocum said. "That was his dynamite that turned the tide back there."

"It will be duly noted in my report." From Captain Tyler's stiffness, Slocum knew he wanted nothing more than to get rid of any civilian who might have witnessed the debacle. The report might record a fantastic victory over the elusive Banded Snake and his warriors, but Slocum knew better. Only pure luck had won the day for the cavalry.

If the last stick of dynamite hadn't started a miniature landslide and blocked the Indians' escape, Tyler would be following Banded Snake all the way to Canada.

"Sir, we found this in their chief's belongings." A sergeant handed Captain Tyler a package wrapped in white paper. Tyler opened it and thumbed through whatever was inside. He handed the package to Slocum and asked, "What do you make of these?"

Slocum was surprised to see a half dozen photographs, mostly of Indians. One was a scenic shot similar to the one he had that Phillip Waddell had taken. Slocum turned the photograph over and peered at the back in the dim twilight.

"Banded Snake must have come across Waddell—Miss Waddell's father," Slocum said, wondering if he needed to ride any farther in search of the photographer. The Ute leader wasn't the kind to let any white man live for long.

Slocum held up the pictures and looked closely at them. Each bore Waddell's name on the back, and he recognized the backgrounds in two others as being the town of Cheyenne. He almost smiled when he saw a photograph of a leering Iron Foot. This cinched it as far as he was concerned.

Banded Snake had taken these from Phillip Waddell, and maybe taken them from his dead body.

"Can I talk with Banded Snake for a minute, Captain?"

"Go on, but make it quick. We're getting out of this pass before it gets much darker."

Slocum went to where the Ute chief sat stolidly astride his pony. Not saying anything for several minutes, Slocum framed his thoughts. Then he asked, "The man who took these photographs. What became of him?" Slocum held up the photographs taken from Banded Snake.

The Indian chief never moved a muscle. Slocum knew better than to rush things. The Indian would answer, or maybe not, and if he did it would be in his own time.

"We traded," Banded Snake said suddenly. "Those amused me. He stole the soul of my enemies."

That was all Slocum was likely to get, but the Ute had said he had traded. More than likely he had given Phillip Waddell his life in exchange for the photographs. Slocum relaxed a mite, knowing the photographer led a charmed existence—or he had more lives than a cat.

Returning to where the captain spoke quietly with three of his non-coms, Slocum waited until Captain Tyler noticed him. Tyler swung around.

"What is it, Slocum?"

"What's going to happen to Moss?" Slocum had other questions but this seemed the one most likely to be answered.

"Behavior such as that exhibited by Lieutenant Moss merits attention by higher authority," Tyler said evasively.

"Can't decide whether to court-martial him for stupidity or give him a medal?" Slocum saw that this covered the only options likely to be followed. "I'd drum him out of the service before he kills more good men."

"Thank you for your counsel, Mr. Slocum." The coldness of the words told Slocum exactly how much his opinion was appreciated or likely to be heeded.

Slocum watched the troopers ride out with their prisoners. George Fourkiller trailed them. The Cherokee slowed and looked down at Slocum, then he smiled broadly and touched the brim of his hat in a sardonic salute. Then he spurred his horse on to join the soldiers.

The darkness quickly swallowed the soldiers. Slocum peered at Waddell's pictures one last time before tucking them into his shirt. Then he went to fetch his horse. He had an hour's ride ahead of him in the dark before finding Ruth Waddell and being able to tell her what he had discovered.

"All these are Father's," Ruth said, eagerly flipping through the photographs. "You took them from the Ute chieftain?"

"That's where they were found," Slocum said. He had downplayed the battle and hadn't mentioned how close the Utes had come to getting away because of the lieutenant's recklessness.

"Does this mean he's . . . dead?" Her voice choked.

"Just the reverse," Slocum said. "Banded Snake must have come across your father. Maybe the Ute was afraid of him because of his camera. Probably not. I reckon your pa traded these pictures to Banded Snake for his freedom. Banded Snake seemed real pleased with the trade because he thought his enemies had lost their souls to your pa's photographs."

"So we continue?" Ruth sounded almost despondent over the notion that her father was still alive and ahead of them.

"As quick as we can," Slocum said. His thoughts kept turning to Bronston being so far ahead of them. "We can be on the other side of the pass by ten o'clock tomorrow morning and on your father's trail by noon."

"We'll find him, won't we, John?" Ruth sounded like a small, frightened child.

"We'll find him," he reassured her. And he silently added, And Bronston will pay in full for all he's done.

18

Slocum and Ruth Waddell got through the littered pass in less than an hour. Slocum rode down the far side of the hill, using the elevation to look around for any sign of an incautious campfire. He saw nothing, which was all he had expected. Spotting the Ute fires and the cavalry's unfortunate bonfires had been a fluke. Getting lucky in such a way twice was out of the question.

"How far north of Cheyenne are we?" asked Ruth as they made their way down a winding path.

"Not far enough," Slocum said. He had chased Bronston and the Utes farther to the west. This path led to Devils Tower. With the map Ruth had created in Cheyenne burned into his memory, he knew exactly where they were and how far they had to travel.

Given the rough countryside, they'd be lucky to make fifty miles in three days.

"Would you prefer to ride on, scouting the trail and allowing me to ride at a slower pace? You might find Father that much sooner."

"No," Slocum said. He didn't want the woman traveling alone in this wilderness. It was getting on to summertime, and the high country had many traps for the unwary. Ruth didn't have sense enough to avoid a grizzly bear and its cubs, or even a puma on the prowl. The mountain lions seldom attacked a human unless provoked. Slocum knew that Ruth was so ignorant she would think it was nothing more than an oversized house cat if she came across one.

"I'm not completely helpless," she said tartly. "I've come this far and done quite well, thank you."

"Bronston is out here somewhere. You'd never stand a chance against him and his men. They're all killers." Slocum spoke slowly; a plan was forming in his head. If he could be sure Bronston was near, he'd make it seem like he was taking Ruth up on her proposal.

What a trap that would be! Bronston couldn't resist coming to capture Phillip Waddell's daughter. Then Slocum would spring his own trap and cut the Union major down where he stood.

He heaved a deep sigh. This was all one tall tale, and he knew it. Bronston was traveling hard and fast to get to Devils Tower, and so must they. The small advantage they had of guessing that Waddell would stop in the meadow to the south of the peak was evaporating day by day.

Phillip Waddell would get his photographs and move on closer to Devils Tower—right where Bronston was heading.

"We'll ride faster," he said. "As we use up our supplies, the mule can travel faster, too. We'll get there."

"John," Ruth said, her voice quivering with emotion. He looked at her and wondered what was going on behind those luminous brown eyes of hers. "I can never thank you for all you've done. Money isn't enough."

"It helps," Slocum said awkwardly, not knowing how to answer. He was captivated by her charms, but he was slave to another master. Revenge drove him harder and faster than any affection for Ruth Waddell ever could.

"We'll find Father. I know it," she said staring straight ahead. Slocum started to agree, then fell silent. Ruth didn't want or need his opinions right now. She was busy convincing herself she wasn't on a wild-goose chase.

They rode in silence for another twenty minutes, then Slocum reined back suddenly. He bent over and peered at the trail. Dismounting, he dropped to a knee and gently pried loose the glinting metallic edge he had seen from horseback.

He held up a photographic plate.

"Father's?" Ruth asked, a flush of excitement rising in her cheeks.

"It's got his name scratched on the back, just like the others," Slocum said. "He sure seems careless with these," Slocum observed.

"He cares only for the few best shots. If he gets a good shot, he tends to ignore the others as he moves on." She smiled in memory of her father's habits. "He might throw away a better shot, but I never saw evidence of it."

"If we could develop this, we'd know where he's been," Slocum said.

"But that's not as important as where he's going."

"And we know this is the right trail."

Slocum walked his horse a few yards, stopping and staring at a pile of dung. It was a few days old from the look of the flies and beetles living in it, and there was more than what a single horse would leave. He walked around the area and found the remains of a large campfire and signs of three or four horses.

Bronston.

"It's the right trail," he agreed.

"I can't go on any more," Ruth said. "We've been riding twelve hours a day for four days, and I'm sick of crossing rivers and climbing mountains."

Slocum wanted to add that it wasn't enough. They made better time than he'd thought when they came down the far side of the pass leaving Tyler and the Utes behind, but it wasn't enough. He was driven and wanted to make one hundred miles a day, if he could. But with Ruth along, that was out of the question. In the time since they'd left Cheyenne, he reckoned they'd traveled a goodly three hundred miles. If it had all been in a straight line, they'd have arrived at Devils Tower by now. Unfortunately, the mountains caused detours and hunts for passes until he was driven to distraction.

"This narrow canyon is making me crazy," she complained. Ruth looked up at the steep sides and shivered.

Slocum rode a few yards ahead and reined back. She came up beside him, not seeing what he had just seen.

"There it is," he said softly. "Devils Tower."

Purpled by haze, the flat-topped tower of rock rose like some powerful titan muscling its way up from the restraining earth.

"Devils Tower," she repeated. "Father!"

Slocum didn't have any trouble keeping the brunette moving that afternoon. If anything, he had to slow the pace to keep a better watch on the trail. He wasn't sure if they had followed the identical route north that Phillip Waddell and Bronston had since he hadn't seen any more recent traces of passage, but the paths were all converging here. Somehow, the majestic flat-topped spire seemed the right place for the meeting Slocum had in mind.

"Wait," he said at just past midday. "The trail's chopped up here." He dismounted and looked around. Unshod ponies had passed through a few days earlier. Wind had rounded the edges of the impressions almost to the point of being invisible, but there were fresher tracks on top of the others.

"Does your father have a couple of supply animals?"

"He rides a horse and has two burros," she said. "He sent a picture of them."

"This is his track," Slocum said with conviction. "Two smaller animals walked along there." He pointed out that portion of the trail for Ruth. "And a horse walked here. You can see a hoofprint only every few yards, but it's there." Slocum looked up and saw how the trail curled gently to the south of Devils Tower.

Ruth's old prospector back in Cheyenne was right on the money.

"What of Major Bronston?" she asked. "Do you see his traces, also?"

"Nothing," Slocum said. That worried him a mite, but not too much at the moment. They could find Phillip Waddell and then worry about the former cavalry major and his men.

They rode at a steady pace for the rest of the afternoon, and found the meadow marked on Ruth's map a few hours before sunset. Slocum held up his hand to stop Ruth. He pointed across the glade to the exact center where a small rise provided a good vantage of the surrounding forest, and an even better view of Devils Tower.

"Father!" Ruth couldn't restrain herself. She dropped the bridle to the mule and her spare horse and raced for Phillip Waddell. Slocum paused to scoop up the reins to keep the animals from wandering off, then followed the galloping woman at a more sedate pace.

Slocum's piercing eyes studied the perimeter of the forest surrounding the green sward for any sign of Bronston or his men. The tranquility was enough to make Slocum think there wasn't a care in the world. He arrived after Ruth had dismounted and rushed to her father, who was aiming his camera at the prominent rise that was Devils Tower.

Dismounting, Slocum staked the horses and mule, then sauntered over.

"She died, Father. She died!" Ruth cried. Tears streamed down her face. "I had to come tell you."

"So?" Phillip Waddell said, turning from his daughter. Slocum saw the anguish on the photographer's face. The man tried to keep it from his daughter. "Rose was so strong. I will miss her terribly." Waddell bent over his camera and fiddled with a knob on the side.

"Whatever will we do without her?" asked Ruth.

"You had done well, Ruth," Waddell said. "We will continue doing well, even if there is a hole in the middle of our lives." The photographer turned and looked at Slocum with an appraising eye. "So, this is the man who helped you?"

"John Slocum, sir," Slocum introduced himself.

"Thank you for bringing Ruth here, even if she has brought such sad news." Waddell seemed to dismiss Slocum immediately. He pulled up a black silk curtain and threw it over his head, burying his face in the rear of the camera. "The light is almost right. Soon, soon it will be perfect!"

Slocum was provoked at the way the man ignored his daughter. Not knowing anything about light, Slocum didn't see why a photograph now was any different from a photograph tomorrow. He went to Ruth and said softly, "Why don't you find your father's camp and get everything set up there?"

"John, it's not like you think," Ruth said in a whisper. "He is so involved in his work; it consumes him." She wiped at her tears but they still left muddy tracks down her cheeks. "Mama's death affects him, but the work takes him away from facing the grief. For the moment. He will mourn her later, after the work is finished."

Slocum shrugged it off. He had seen men break down and bawl like a calf without its mother. He had seen other men react to tragedy as if it meant nothing. Then there was just about every shade in between. Phillip Waddell would find his own way of bereavement.

"Your daughter's gone through hell getting to you with this news," Slocum said.

"I appreciate your efforts on her behalf." Waddell pulled back and studied Devils Tower. What he saw there was beyond Slocum's reckoning.

Slocum shifted his weight from foot to foot. "We fought through a band of Utes."

Waddell laughed. "Banded Snake? The old fraud. He pretended to be hard as nails, but he was as interested in my work as most people."

Slocum started to tell Waddell what the Ute had done, then stopped. The photographer was completely wrapped up in his work. Anything beyond it was beyond his pale. God protected fools and drunks—and maybe self-absorbed photographers.

"We tracked you down from people you talked to in Cheyenne," Slocum said, angling around to the question he wanted answered most. "And Iron Foot. I talked with him."

"Another old fraud. He will be in my picture book. Iron Foot will rival anything Mathew Brady recorded." Waddell laughed harshly. "That fool's gone bankrupt. Did Ruth tell you? Congress didn't act to buy his National Gallery, and Brady was forced to give up both his New York and Washington galleries." Waddell walked around, his eyes focused on Devils Tower.

"He ought to have given individual credit to his photographers. We could have helped, but no, he drove us out. The fool! Burgess & Company took over his business."

"That's fine," Slocum said, still working around to the question burning like a fever in his brain. "It's always nice to see a competitor fail."

"There's no competition," Waddell said. "I'm better. This collection will prove it to the world. I do more than simple portraits. Even during the War Between the States, I proved that!"

Slocum didn't know how to couch his question in the right terms so he just came out and asked. "We've been dogged all the way by a former Union cavalry officer named Bronston. David James Bronston. Why's he want you so bad?"

Waddell turned and looked at Slocum. "Bronston?" he asked. "I don't know any Bronston." Phillip Waddell turned back and chortled at the light levels descending on Devils Tower.

Slocum simply stared at the man. How could Waddell not know Bronston when the former major had moved heaven and earth to find him—and to try and kill him?

19

"You must know him," pressed Slocum. He couldn't believe Bronston was after Waddell for no reason. There had to be a reason, and Phillip Waddell had to know what it was.

"Don't know any Union officers. Not well, at any rate, and not since the war," he amended, peering under his black silk shroud through the lens again. "Perfect. In a little while, this will be the perfect shot. Setting sun, the hues just right, shadows playing along the base and the fluted rocks on the sides. Devils Tower rises 1280 feet, you know. Straight up from the plains, and no man's ever climbed it. I reckon I'll be about the first to photograph it."

"David James Bronston," Slocum said. "A tad less than my height, thin, face like the blade of a hatchet, has a sergeant named Dickensen following him around like some kind of attack dog. He must have been cashiered from the cavalry. Maybe both of them. I heard tell he was sentenced to the Detroit Penitentiary."

"For what?"

"I don't know," Slocum said. "You might know." He was puzzled that Waddell insisted he didn't know Bronston. Bronston's drive for revenge knew no bounds and Waddell was ignorant of it. Such determination and rage didn't come out of nowhere.

Waddell came out from under his camera, pursed his lips, and bit down hard on the lower one, thinking hard. "Might he have been court-martialed for cruelty to his own men?"

"He's the kind who would," Slocum said, hope rising. "Do you remember him now?"

"Not really, though there is a possible incident that happened near the end of the war. I was taking pictures of a minor skirmish for Mathew Brady. He was busy shooting portraits of a general at the time and had left the real work to several of us. The Union forces won an easy victory, except for one portion of the battlefield. The officer in charge of a cavalry unit—a major—disciplined his men quite harshly. Four died after he had them lashed for failing to hold their line. I took pictures of the aftermath. Bloody. Very ugly affair."

"And Bronston was the commanding officer?"

"Don't recollect the man's name. Heard tell my photographs helped convict him. Deserved it. Beat those boys to death. Worst thing I ever photographed." Waddell shook his head and made a few minor adjustments on his tripod.

Slocum heaved a deep sigh. That must be the explanation. Phillip Waddell had helped convict Bronston because of photographs taken of his brutal disciplining of his own troopers. If he had been stripped of rank and sent to prison, that explained much of what had gone on.

Slocum started to ask Waddell a few more questions but the photographer had buried his head under the black silk curtain once more and was oblivious to everything else in the world. He emerged, with a broad smile on his face.

"This will be the perfect shot."

And it was, but not the kind Phillip Waddell had meant. A bullet sang over the meadow and hit the photographer in the back of the head. He pitched forward, dead before he hit the ground.

A loud scream from the direction of Waddell's camp punctuated the rifle's report. It died as swiftly as it had started, and Slocum went cold inside.

"Ruth!" he called.

Slocum vaulted into his saddle and galloped hard across the meadow, staying low to keep from becoming a target like Waddell. He hit the ground running with his Colt Navy drawn and ready. But he was alone. The camp was a shambles and a piece of torn skirt showed where Ruth had put up a fight. Slocum calmed down and made a quick circuit of the camp, just to be sure Bronston and the others had left with their victim.

He tried to reconstruct what had happened. The ground was soft and the grass fresh, leaving easily read spoor. Two men had waited in hiding, maybe watching as Ruth went about her chores in adding their supplies to those of her father's. Slocum found a shiny brass cartridge from the rifle used to kill Waddell.

"Bronston," he said, estimating the distance and skill required to kill Waddell. He would have thought the former major would have wanted to torture Waddell, to see Waddell's pain-racked face and make it a more personal revenge. Then Slocum knew what Bronston's revenge would be.

Bronston had Ruth.

Slocum went to his saddlebags and got out spare ammunition. He wanted to be ready for a long siege. Taking his Winchester from the saddle boot, he made sure the magazine was full. Loaded for big game, Slocum went hunting.

The track through the wooded area wasn't hard to follow. Slocum went cautiously, knowing Bronston wasn't so careless as to think Slocum would turn tail and run when Waddell was killed and Ruth kidnapped. He dropped to one knee when he came to a glade. The tracks led smack across a muddy area, warning Slocum of a trap.

Bronston was no one's fool. He had to know Slocum would be after him.

Slocum chafed at the need to wait for a spell to draw them out, but he was glad he did. He sat better than ten minutes before he saw movement at the right side of the clearing. He looked to the other side and immediately found a sniper. If he had blundered into the glade where there wasn't a chance for cover, he'd have been caught in a deadly cross fire.

He made his way to the east, moving silently until he came upon the sniper fidgeting impatiently and waiting for his prey. Slocum showed him the meaning of patience by slamming his rifle butt into the back of the man's head. He pitched forward, but he let out a loud grunt as he fell.

"Josh, what's up?" came the cry from the other side of the glade.

Slocum grunted again, then moaned, hoping he was bull-throated enough to duplicate the fallen man's timbre. He lifted his rifle, aimed and waited. His finger came back in a smooth movement, the Winchester jumped, and another man died. Slocum looked down at the man unconscious at his feet and considered simply shooting him, too, then decided against it. He had a fighting chance now. He had to take it. Slocum used the rifle butt on the back of the man's head a final time to be sure he wouldn't come along later and try to backshoot him.

Bronston would be waiting for a shot or two, thinking his men had ambushed Slocum. He might not expect to see the one he thought to be dead waltz into his camp.

Slocum hurried around the glade, picked up the trail easily and rushed onward. He heard voices through the forest and recognized them both.

"Josh got him, Major. That boy's a crack shot."

"Go be sure, Dickensen," Bronston said. "Slocum has proven slippery before."

"Not this time. He'll be all het up over her, sniffing after her like a buck in rut." Dickensen laughed harshly.

"You might be right. Check." Bronston's voice carried the snap of command.

"Yes, sir, right away," said the former sergeant.

"Oh, Sergeant," called Bronston. "One more thing."

"What is it, sir?" Dickensen sounded a bit surly at being sent out on such a minor errand.

"I've had my revenge on the photographer. You may continue with his daughter after you return. And tell Josh he can have a turn at her, also."

Slocum heard Dickensen's lewd laugh and Ruth's frightened sobs. He almost rushed forward but held back. He was getting the men apart, and that made taking them out all the easier. To reveal himself now would give them the upper hand.

Slocum tried to see Bronston through the thick undergrowth but couldn't. He considered simply walking into the camp and shooting the man, but that would leave Dickensen at his back. Better to snip off the leaves on this weed before going for the roots.

Like a ghost Slocum floated through the trees less than ten paces behind the cavalry sergeant. Dickensen never heard him as the distance closed. Slocum paused when Dickensen called out to his fallen comrade. When he got no answer, he drew his pistol, and looked around.

Slocum dived for cover with his rifle at the ready. If Dickensen had seen him, he would have fired. But Slocum wanted to make this kill as quiet as possible to keep from alerting Bronston. As long as Bronston held a gun and was in camp with Ruth, she could suffer greatly.

"Josh! Where the hell are you?" Dickensen thought the man was funning him, but that notion would change quickly enough when he found the body.

Slocum moved closer, his hand sweaty on the rifle stock. He usually didn't get nervous before he killed a man, but he was this time. Too much was riding on a silent kill.

Dickensen spun unexpectedly and saw Slocum. He lifted his pistol to get off a shot. Slocum rushed him. He brought up the barrel of his rifle and smashed it under Dickensen's gun hand. Metal crunched hard into bone and sent the sergeant's six-shooter flying. Slocum's luck gave out then. When the six-gun hit the ground, it discharged.

"Major!" roared Dickensen as Slocum closed in on him.

Using the rifle as a lever, Slocum forced Dickensen back hard. The sergeant tried to backpedal fast and stumbled. Slocum landed on him with the Winchester's barrel coming down in a bar across the man's exposed throat. Dickensen grabbed the rifle with both hands and tried to push it up. Slocum used his full weight, his full strength, and more than an ounce of anger to drive the barrel down into Dickensen's Adam's apple.

The sergeant began to choke. Slocum felt the life ebbing from the man's body. He didn't lessen the pressure until Dickensen lay blue-faced and unmoving.

Panting harshly, Slocum rocked back on his heels. He had eliminated two of Bronston's men. That left only the leader, and he had been warned by the accidental discharge from Dickensen's pistol and the shout.

Or had he?

The first shot had been misinterpreted as being Slocum's end. Maybe the major had so much confidence in his sergeant that he thought the second shot ended Slocum's life. Slocum didn't have much else to play on at the moment. He had to be bold and take the risk.

He checked his rifle and wondered if it had been damaged in the fight with Dickensen. He couldn't tell—and that worried him. He discarded it and relied on his Colt. The trusty six-shooter wouldn't betray him.

Making his way back through the wooded area, Slocum circled and came to Bronston's camp from the opposite side Dickensen had left. He stepped forward slowly and saw the cavalry major sitting with his back to Slocum and a rifle across his lap. Slocum caught his breath. The muzzle was pointed in Ruth's direction. The brunette sat shaking in fear.

"Why are you doing this to me?" she asked Bronston.

"He was responsible for me being reduced in rank and put in a cage," Bronston said. "Him and his damned photographs."

"I don't understand what you mean," Ruth said. "I have never met you before Kansas City. I—"

"Shut up," Bronston said harshly. "You just happened to get in the way, though it makes for better revenge. Your father's dead. I shot him with this rifle." Bronston patted the weapon in his lap. "One shot and he died."

"What about me?" Ruth asked.

"You're part of my revenge. I had thought I wanted to torture your father, make him beg for mercy, let him know a fraction of what I suffered for six years while I rotted in prison. But I saw him in the field and knew that wasn't what I wanted to do."

"You want to torture me?"

"Yes," he said simply.

Slocum wasn't aware of making a sound but the major stiffened slightly and lifted the rifle, pressing it firmly into Ruth's temple.

"You killed Sergeant Dickensen, didn't you, Slocum?"

"Yes," Slocum said softly. "You're next."

"What was it?" Bronston asked, turning around without ever taking the rifle away from the brunette's head. "What strange loyalty drives you? Do you love her? I know your kind. You can't love a woman that much."

"The watch," Slocum said. "You stole my watch."

"That?" Bronston's eyebrows shot up in amazement. "You said that before. I don't believe you. There must be more. Money. She's paying you some fabulous amount of money to save her."

"I don't care if she gives me one red cent," Slocum said. He widened his stance. He could get his Colt Navy out and fire in the blink of an eye, but he needed a break. He could kill Bronston any time he wanted, but Bronston would also kill Ruth.

"The watch?" Bronston shook his head in disbelief. "I do declare. That's about the most outrageous thing I've ever heard."

"It was my brother's. It's all I have to remember him."

"Unbelievable," Bronston said. The major's shoulders tensed and told Slocum death was coming his way. As Bronston swung the rifle around, Slocum went for his six-shooter. His hand flew to his cross-draw holster and whipped out the heavy pistol. The first round was on its way before Bronston finished turning.

The second round caught the former major in the middle of the chest just as he pulled the rifle's trigger.

The third round tore through his face and sent him tumbling backward. The single shot he had triggered missed Slocum by a country mile.

"John!" gasped out Ruth. "You saved me."

He ignored her and went to the fallen officer's side. He opened Bronston's tattered military jacket and fumbled inside. Again he found the watch with its heavy gold chain attached. This time Slocum pulled it free and put it back where it belonged, in his own vest pocket. Only then did he see to the woman.

"Is it true? Did he kill Father?"

"Afraid so," Slocum said, freeing her from her bonds. She rubbed her wrists to get the circulation back and looked stricken. "But this is the end of the road. Bronston's dead. So is Dickensen and the man with him. Seems everybody but us has turned up dead."

She clutched him and buried her face into his chest. She shook and sobbed but Slocum didn't feel any tears turning his shoulder damp. Ruth was past the point where that would be possible. Later, maybe, when the full impact of everything sunk in, then she would cry.

But not now.

"Take me back to camp, John. I . . . I want to see him one last time."

"I can take care of everything. It wasn't too pretty," he said, remembering how Bronston's bullet had caught Phillip Waddell square in the back of the head. The rifle slug would have ripped off the photographer's face.

"There's nothing more for me to do. I want to see him buried. Out there, in the middle of that meadow."

Silently they returned to where Phillip Waddell had set up his camera. The man lay sprawled gracelessly beside the tripod. He was as much of a mess as Slocum had thought he would be. Ruth stood for a moment and stared down at him. She muttered something Slocum didn't catch.

"We'd better get him into the ground," Slocum said, casting a wary eye to the sky. The sun was setting, and the vultures were starting to circle. He didn't care if they feasted on Bronston and the others. Slocum just hoped the buzzards wouldn't choke. But he felt he owed something to Phillip Waddell—or to his daughter. A decent burial was the least he could do.

"I'll see that you are well compensated for this, John," Ruth said in a dull voice.

"We can talk about that later," he said. He got to digging. It took Slocum almost an hour to dig a decently deep grave. He heard the howling of coyotes and wolves in the distance, and knew it would have to be deep and weighted on top with stones to keep them from getting at Waddell's body.

He rolled the photographer into the grave and quickly shoved back the dirt. On the mound he placed as many stones as he could gather. Wiping the sweat from his forehead he asked, "Do you want to say a few words over the grave?"

Ruth Waddell had buried her head under the black silk cloth and was peering through the lens at Devils Tower.

"The light is about perfect. This is the shot he wanted. Devils Tower just at sundown."

"Your father," Slocum said, exasperated. "What about him?"

"This will be his epitaph," Ruth said. She pulled back a sliding metal plate, clicked the shutter, counted slowly, then replaced the metal sheet. "This will be all the tribute to his memory he needs."

Slocum watched in silence as Ruth Waddell took the camera off the tripod, bundled the camera up in a case, and walked slowly back toward camp. He glanced at the blood-colored Devils Tower, shook his head and followed.

If you enjoyed this book, subscribe now and get...

TWO FREE

A $7.00 VALUE—